ELLIE QUIN SERIES:

THE LEGEND OF ELLIE QUIN

Published by Grrr Books, 2012
© Alex Scarrow, 2012
© Cover Design and Cover Image
Alex Scarrow, 2012

First Edition

ISBN: 978-0-9575160-0-7

The Legend of Ellie Quin

By

Alex Scarrow

[Begin….]

[An Audio fragment]:

'Oh God,' we can hear a girl's voice whimpering. 'Oh crud, Hufty, I think she's dead! Or, she's, like, *dying*. I'm sure she is. I…I can feel her blood all over my lap. It's all over me. Oh no…please don't leave me alone in here, please don't die!'

The girl's voice falters. We can hear the rustle of her moving around.

'Wake up! Can you hear me? Please…oh, crud, please don't die on me!'

The sound of the girl crying, and there's something else - the sound of a deep, booming rumble in the background, getting progressively louder.

'I really can't do this on my own. Not without *you*,' the girl whispers.

We hear the sound of sobbing and movement of some kind, the rustling of clothes, perhaps a shifting of position.

'I'm just…I'm nothing. I'm stupid and lost…and I want to go back home.'

The deep bass rumbling is getting louder and causing the recording to distort and crackle. It sounds like something large is gathering momentum.

'Please...don't die, don't leave me alone here. Ple-e-e-ease!!!!'

We hear the sound of somebody fumbling with a switch, then silence.

[End of audio fragment]:

OMNIPEDIA:
[Human Universe: digital encyclopedia]

Article: 'The Legend of Ellie Quin'

The recording you just listened to was taken from an audio file fragment; one of only a few verified recordings of her voice left in existence today. She was believed to have been only about twenty years of age when she made that entry on her voice diary at the beginning of the thirty-first century...*over 700 years ago*. She was known to have made regular voice-diaries of her incredible life, though, sadly too few fragments of these recordings have survived.

To this very day no one has been able to work out exactly *who* she was referring to, whom she was with then; who *exactly* was dying in her arms when she made that recording. We shall never know. In addition, no one has ever managed to determine who the intended recipient - Hufty - was. A friend? A lover? A relative?

Just two of the many mysteries that surround the amazing legend of Ellie Quin. Hers is the story of an ordinary young woman who not only ended up altering the course of history…but ultimately saving mankind from itself.

What we do know is that she started out as a farmer's daughter on a remote planet in the Seventh Veil, called 'Harpers Reach'.

User Comment > Anonymous
That it? That's all there is on her? Totally Crud article!

User Comment > Liz T-Pup
If she's such a big legend, if she saved the entire human race? How come there aren't whole planets named after her? Or cities and stuff? She's a myth. She never existed. Itsa-hoax.

User Comment > GoldenNexus
This Omni-article entry is rubbish, way-y-y too sketchy. I want to know more about her. I heard her name once on a history datachip. Never thought to read up on her though.

User Comment > Random DittoBoy
If you want to know more about her…go build a time machine and travel back to the year three thousand, or whenever it was.

Anyway…who cares about someone who died 700 years ago? Boring.

To read more of **34,567,984** User Comments – Register with Omnipedia through your planetary digi-stream service provider.

CHAPTER 1

'Hufty, I'm sorry it's been so long since I last recorded a letter to you. It's been really busy here on the farm. Dad's had me and Shona, and even Ted, working on the weeds. I hate those damn plants. They're...they're such a pain in the butt. You know I told you they're kind of half plant, half animal? Well, they have these pods with little spikes on, a bit like a hairbrush, and if they decide they don't like what you're up to, they smack you with it... and quite hard too. Ted seems to have a way with the weeds, they don't seem to mind too much when he re-beds them. Shona doesn't do too bad either. But they've damn well got it in for me. I mean, they must re-e-eally despise me. I've got welts on the back of my hand and all the way up my arms from this morning. I'd love to get away from here some day.'

Ellie paused the voice-diary as she heard a rumbling overhead. She looked up into the peach colored midday sky to see, at high-altitude, a freighter heading due south. The glinting metal of its hull shimmered in the

6

heat. It left a vapor trail behind it that remained in the sky undisturbed by wind; a long sharply defined white line pointing towards New Haven.

From where she sat, Ellie could see the glow of New Haven at night even though it was a hundred and thirty miles away. Sometimes, even in the daytime, if humidity was low, she fancied she could just about see the spectral reflection of the top of the city's enormous enviro-dome on the horizon. It would flicker and undulate like a mirage. Not today though, humidity had brought visibility down.

She watched the freighter arc across the sky. It would be cutting through the uppermost layer of atmosphere, up where the troposphere begins to become space and the curvature of the horizon is just about discernible. It would stay high until the final approach to the city. She patiently watched it until it began to fade and merge with the heat-quivering horizon. Just as it was fading from view, she saw the flicker of the entry shields as it began its descent into the denser atmosphere below and it made its final vector into New Haven's port.

There was nothing left to see up above. She looked down at the farm; three large plexitex agri-domes, each containing roughly an acre of those mean-spirited tubweeds. The agri-domes were arranged around a much smaller dome in the centre – home.

Ellie liked it up here; the *overlook*, a craggy rock that emerged from the clay-like soil of Harpers Reach like the desperate, reaching hand of a drowning man. She liked it because of the height and the view and because up here she felt that bit closer to the sky and the stars at night. Sometimes, very occasionally, smaller ships and personal transport vessels would skim over low enough to feel the downdraft as they passed by.

'That rumbling sound?' she continued, 'that was a freighter coming into New Haven. They come by two or three times a day. One day Hufty, and soon…I'm heading that way myself.'

Ellie switched off the diary.

Her oxygen mask was killing her. She found the plastic rim bit into the bridge of her nose after a while. She pulled it off and held the mask in her hands as she loosened

8

the straps slightly. She took a tentative mouthful of air. It wasn't bad today, quite dense. On occasional days you could breathe atmosphere for a short while before needing to resort to using a mask. If you were really lucky and hit a rich pocket of oxygen you could go several minutes. Eventually though, you would need to use breathing apparatus or you'd keel over. Thousands of miles away, towards the north polar region, several enormous refineries were slowly working on turning the atmosphere oxygen-rich. Built over a hundred and fifty years ago they would probably be running another fifty before they were no longer needed. And then, of course farmers, case in point - her father - would be out of business.

Ellie rubbed the sore patches on either side of her nose and put the mask back on gently, then started down towards the farm, kicking up dust in her wake and leaving a rust-red plume behind her like the freighter's drifting jet stream in the peach-hued sky.

She let herself into the northern bio-dome. The Quin family referred to this one as 'Betsy'. Her father, Jacob Quin, had let each of his three kids name a dome. Ted had got in first with 'Booster' as the name chosen for his dome. He named it after a character from one of those stupid morning holo-toob cartoon shows; all 'splosions and over-the-top violence.

Ted was, to be fair, your typical seven year old boy.

So, because Ted had got in first with 'Booster' Dad - for some reason - decided that all three agri-domes should have nicknames beginning with 'B'. Shona, only two years older than Ted, and still perfectly capable of enjoying the mindless banality of children's toob, had gone with 'Buttball', a character from a rival cartoon.

Ellie named her dome after Betsy Boomalackah, a girl the same age as her - nineteen - and making zillions of creds out of music that parents planet-wide hated, and kids loved for that very reason.

It was hot. Inside Betsy it was always hot and humid. The airborne moisture hit her like a wet wall. Ellie peeled off her mask and hung it and the accompanying O2 cylinder on a hook beside the door.

Ahead of her, like a grim rank of soldiers standing to attention, grew row after row of tubweeds. Each, it seemed, with a personal grudge against her. She slipped on a pair of elbow length rubber gloves and grabbed a bucket of fertilizer pellets.

'Okay you miserable weeds, chow time.'

She proceeded down the first row, shoveling a handful of pellets at the base of each plant's thick corded stem. They swayed silently, the leaves rustling softly, sensing it was feed time and impatient for their nutrients.

Ellie had once seen a thing called a 'movie', one of those flickering two dimensional things people used to watch way back in the dark ages of the twenty-first century. The movie she had seen was called 'The Day of the Triffids'. The similarity was genuinely striking, not in just their appearance; the sturdy, corded trunk, the broccoli-like florets at the top from which a long agile stem emerged and culminated in a spine-covered pod, but also in their crappy attitude.

Tubweeds had three very distinct properties. Firstly, they possessed a very simple intelligence. Dad said they were roughly as smart as a housefly. Experiments carried out on the plant indicated that at a very basic level it was aware of, and reacted to light, sound, motion and heat.

Secondly, they smelled appalling. She had once tried to describe the smell to Hufty, the closest she had got was 'they sort of smell like meat and mint at the same time'.

Thirdly, their unique proficiency at absorbing carbon dioxide and monoxide and turning it into oxygen output; the process known as 'respiration'. A well known statistic amongst tubweed farmers was that, during a growth-spurt, a single tubweed could produce enough oxygen to sustain seven adult humans.

The plant beside Ellie had begun to grow impatient and a tentacle reached inside the bucket. Ellie smacked it sharply with her spade. It smacked her back with its pod. Even through the thick rubber gloves the spikes hurt.

'Right, you think you're so clever? No pellets for you today.'

The tubweed seemed to wilt slightly. Ellie continued down the row, shoveling pellets onto the soil.

CHAPTER 2

'Come on, concentrate Ellie.'

'I'm trying to, but this is so-o-o boring.'

'It's not boring, and you've got exams coming up, so try and stay a little focused, okay?'

Sean Eltwood held Ellie with a gaze she imagined he thought was stern, commanding. In fact it was nothing of the sort. Ellie stared longingly back at Sean's almost feminine brown eyes, and studied the remarkable angularity of his jaw line. She imagined him in the black and white military camouflage of the Colonial Marines, stepping cautiously through an exotic alien jungle, pulse rifle held at the ready. She switched fantasies; Sean in formal dress uniform extending a spotless white-gloved hand and beckoning her to come to him. His wholesome smile and dreamy long-lashed eyes framed by the black peak of his parade ground cap.

Mmmmmm...

'Ellie?'

Snap out of it girl.

'Focus? Yes, certainly. Focus.' She nodded sternly. 'I'm focusing.'

Sean was twenty; just over a year older than her. His family lived in a similar farm just a few miles away. They grew a far less troublesome cash crop, proto-meat plants. He had finished home-schooling and had been eagerly looking forward to starting college in New Haven. But then his name came up in the Colonial Marine draft lottery and he was due to head off to join the army soon to begin training.

Sean was ecstatic when he first found out.

The last few weeks since he'd been notified had been one long tap dance. They trained off-world, and that alone - getting off world - was worth the price of admission as far as Sean was concerned. The accompanying holo-vid that came with the draft slip listed the worlds that would be visited during the training period. It proudly claimed that every marine would be capable of fighting proficiently in high and low gravity environments, capable of drop-ship, jet-pod and sky-chute deployments and, in addition, would learn a valuable tech skill by the end of boot camp. All of a sudden Sean's long-held goal of attending college in New

Haven had seemed a comparatively unexciting and parochial ambition.

'So, when do you leave?'

'The Big Freezer's due to hit our orbit in about four months,' he replied.

The recruitment ship for the Colonial Defense Force toured the colony worlds of the Seventh Veil every seven or eight years. It was big, very big; incapable of planetary landings. It was designed to carry up to ten thousand recruits, each housed in their own cryogenic sarcophagus; a huge freight ship carrying a payload of frozen recruits. The journey back to GL5-D (the rather un-poetic name for the planet that was home to the Colonial Defense Force) would take about a month. But a month of three meals a day for ten thousand hungry mouths validated putting the new recruits on ice for the short duration.

'I bet you're excited. I mean, just getting off-world alone would do it for me. But to think of all the other places you're going to see?'

'Yup, it's going to be double-great,' Sean smiled. 'And, you know, the marines are a mixed gender regiment.'

Ellie knew. He didn't have to sound quite so gleeful about that. 'Good for you.'

'Just like college, only better. Meet chicks, play with guns, see crazy new worlds, get paid…there really is a God,' Sean looked heavenward and winked.

'When you finish your tour of duty…eight years, right? I'll be twenty-seven.'

'Yuh, I know.'

'Weird that, huh? We'll both be in our late-20's.' She stared at him. A little too long. A little too intent. He looked away, his cheeks prickled with color. 'Uh, yeah, I s'pose.'

Nice going, Ellie. Try and keep cool…remember? Cool. Not too grabby?

Not long now. He was going soon. How many more math lessons would he be coming over for? Not many. Sean had things to do to get ready for the Freezer. She'd been half toying with the idea of taking what was likely to be one of the last chances she had left and reaching out for him, planting her lips, firm and unambiguous on his, and declaring she'd been quietly burning for him since he'd started coming over to help out with the math. That, or just keeping a lid on it. Accepting this - whatever this was - was just not destined to happen.

He looked up at Ellie awkwardly. 'Hey, who knows? Maybe *you'll* get drafted.'

'I'm never, ever, that lucky.'

'You never know. It's a large universe. There's usually trouble kicking off somewhere that they need soldiers going in and kicking-'

'I just want to get off-world, like you. See some things, you know? Visit at least a fraction of this cosmos before I shrivel up and die of old age. It's not like I want a war. Want to kill anything.'

'Well, yeah…killing stuff isn't high up on my list either.'

'But meeting chicks holding big guns is, apparently.'

Sean couldn't help an impish grin. 'Sorry Ellie, I know you're…umm…that you *like* me. And I like you too, but-'

But? *Did he just say that?* 'But' was the polite version of a gentle slap.

'But not,' *her* cheeks were prickling now. 'But not like...*that*.'

'I...uh...' He shuffled. Looked down at his hands. 'Not really.'

Ellie felt her stomach lurch. Sick. Why? It's not like he was dumping her. He taught her domestic arithmetic. That's it. Oh yeah, and occasionally they shared a laugh, a nudge, a playful dig in the ribs. But this was never anything more than that.

'I thought...' she could hear her voice trembling. 'I thought maybe we were...well, you know? I just thought there was *something*?'

'Ellie, I'm sorry. I like you. You know I do. But...but...'

'Will you stop saying that?' She snatched up her homework. 'Crud! What are you saying sorry for anyway? I'm, you know, I'm fine!' Her voice was doing that thing when she got angry, nervous, emotional - going squeaky. 'I'm happy for you, actually! And glad I won't have to continue suffering your appalling teaching skills for much longer.' She got up and headed for the door. She could feel her face growing hot with embarrassment.

'Where are you going, Ellie? We haven't finished dom-tech yet.'

'I'm...I need to change the filter in Betsy.'

Ellie slid open the door and left her habi-cube.

He sat in silence for a while, half expecting her to return a moment later with a playful 'gotcha' grin. But no.

He looked around Ellie's habi-cube as he awaited her return. For the first time it occurred to him how little she had. The room belonging to a girl of nineteen, nearly twenty should have more in it. It ought to look like a cross between a stuffed-toy factory and a cosmetics store. Ellie's cabin was stark. A bed, a storage cabinet, a desk, and one stuffed toy, a tartan patterned dog she called 'Johnny'. He knew her Dad paid her pocket money for the chores she did on the farm, but he was damned if he knew what she spent it on. He saved the files they had been working on and turned off the writing tablet.

CHAPTER 3

Ellie sat in a quiet nook of Betsy, well away from the stirring tubweeds. This was her corner of the world, her domain - a wobbly wicker chair and a small glow lamp. She could hear the irritating twittering voices of yet another cartoon on the holo-toob echoing through from the domestic dome, and the guffaw of Ted and Shona as, presumably, another unfortunate character was squashed, diced or blasted into space.

And Sean? Probably he'd just say goodbye to her parents and let himself out.

She looked up at the plexitex ceiling of Betsy. It was dark outside. The sky a rich and deep purple, divided by a golden misty slash; the gas clouds of the nearby Seventh Veil. To the south the faintest tinge of blue-green on the horizon. The glow of New Haven.

There was a thumping sound coming from the tubweed beds. It was, no doubt, the frisky one from earlier on that afternoon taking out hunger-induced frustration on its neighbors. She reached down and grabbed a handful of fertilizer pellets from the bucket and threw it out into the darkness in the rough direction of the misbehaving plant. There was a gentle rustling of leaves and tentacles. She didn't care too much if the damn plant got its meal or not, or whether another had managed to scoop an extra helping, the thumping had stopped.

Ellie was angry with herself; angry with so many dregging-bloody-things at the same time, she didn't know which way to spit venom first. That Sean now knew for certain she had - yes, a girly-wirly crush on him…well, maybe that was just more embarrassing than annoying. Sean was a good guy. He wouldn't brag about it to anyone. Mind you, what was there to brag about? She was hardly catch of the century; a scrawny yard stick with long and lank hair, a plain face and welt marks on her hands and wrists.

She was angry that he was getting away. Yes, that hurt. Envy then; he was getting a chance to go off-world, to see that large universe and the closest she was ever going to get was looking at the stars, watching inbound freighters stitch lines across the sky.

Colonial plot 452; this tatty cluster of dusty agri-domes bang in the middle of this flat, dry, baked-mud world, Harpers Reach. And what was that but a mud-ball planet on the edge of Nebula Cirrus 5, otherwise known as the Seventh Veil. A sparsely populated and generally uninteresting region of space; a little piece of nowhere.

'This damn farm, this is my universe,' she muttered to herself. 'This is all it'll ever be.'

'Not necessarily.'

She spun around in her chair. The canes creaked with the sudden movement. Sean stood in the dark beyond the light thrown out by the glow lamp.

'Sorry Ellie, I wasn't spying, I just wondered whether you were coming back to finish up on your study session.'

'Don't worry, Dad will still pay you,' she replied testily.

'Hey, I'm not worried about that. Can I sit with you?'

She thumbed her lip in the dark. 'Sure...yes, why not?

Sean walked over to her and found an old crate nearby. He pulled it up beside her, sat down and leaned back to look at the sky.

22

Ellie settled back in her chair and followed his gaze.

'If you follow the line of the Veil to the end, the thin end?...the second bright star in is GL-5. The colonial marine planet, GL5-D orbits that,' he said.

'Catchy name.'

He laughed.

They sat in silence with only the distant sound of Ted's quacking laughter and the rustling weeds.

'You're going to see and experience a lot of wonderful things,' Ellie said, trying to keep her voice steady. Going for something that sounded less like tearsome-wallflower-rebuffed.

'I know. I'm really lucky that I got a draft ticket.'

'Is there anything you'll miss here on Harpers Reach?'

'What? You mean apart from coming over here and trying to get basic math to stick in that goopy head of yours?'

Ellie chuckled. Sean wasn't going to miss her, but it was nice of him to crack that funny anyway.

'Not much else that I'll miss I guess. Maybe my folks. But I'll tell you what. I've got to admit I'm not looking forward to being frozen. They say in cryo-suspension that you're not really asleep, just kind of slowed down, so that everything outside your pod seems to happen incredibly quickly like a speeded up holo-film. I don't like the idea that you're aware of everything going on but can't do anything. Like some insect trapped in amber. Know what I mean? You're, like, stuck in this see-through shell and there's these things going on outside.'

Ellie's gaze drifted to the pale glow in the far away sky above New Haven.

Yeah, I know what you mean.

'There was this guy in cryo who survived when his freighter blew up…asteroid impact or something. But he saw it all happen. Okay, he saw it happen in funky speed-o-vision, but he was aware of it all happening. The ship breaking up, explosions in the cargo hold, the hull ripping open…and then all of a sudden spinning in space. And he knew he was screwed, but just couldn't do anything about it. Knowing that he would just carry on spinning until the power supply eventually ran dry. I think that was on the toob news a while back.'

'And they found him?'

'Yup, he was out floating around for several weeks. They thawed him out and the guy was okay but hysterical. Understandably.'

'Scary.'

'Uhuh…I think he sold the rights or something and they're making a holo-film of it. I guess it turned out alright for him in the end.'

'Do you think you'll do any fighting?'

'I don't think so, Ellie. It's mostly a peaceful universe out there. Nothing much to do. Most of the alien cultures in our universe seem to be happy to simply muddle along with ours and trade. If you're not into fighting, it's a great time to be a soldier.'

'What about that new encounter? The one that happened last year?'

'I dunno, it's not been in the news much has it? Last I heard, they seemed to be very aloof, but not threatening. Just a very quiet and spiritual race, I guess. The army seems to be more like a police force these days…the occasional terrorist group, but mostly minding that everyone's being good and not breaking any laws.'

'Sean…it's not fair. You're so lucky to get away from this godforsaken place.'

He couldn't find a reply that felt right. They sat in awkward silence for a while. Sean had something on his mind, the reason he'd decided to come out and speak to her in the first place.

'Ellie?…When exactly were you planning on running away from home?'

Her chair creaked in the darkness. She said nothing.

'Well?'

He could hear Ellie fidgeting uncomfortably.

'How do you know?' she asked eventually.

'Just a lucky guess. And the fact you've been hoarding your chore-money haven't you?'

By the faint light he saw her pull a face. Heard the soft thwack of a fist against a thigh.

'Ellie? When were you planning to go?'

'Soon. After my birthday.'

'New Haven?'

'Yes.'

She turned to face him. In the green glow of the lamp he could see she looked nervous. 'Please don't tell anyone.'

'You can't just run off like that…without telling your Mum and Dad where you're going.'

'I will tell them…when I get settled and sorted out.'

'It's not going to be that easy. New Haven's a rough place. A *really* rough place.'

'I can get a job.'

'That's what I'm worried about. There are jobs and there are jobs. If you know what I mean?

'I'll work something out.'

Silent. The stirring of tubweeds, the burbling of the toob in the family dome.

'Listen Ellie, I won't tell anyone if you promise to wait a little longer. Why don't you hang on here for a couple more years? Grow up a bit more and then try out city life, uh?'

'Because I'll go mad, that's why. Because I can't face the drudge of being a farm girl any longer. Every day the same old routine, and every night sitting out there and seeing the freighters pass in the sky, the glow of New Haven. Even seeing the faint twinkle of ships entering and leaving orbit and the flicker of light as they go into hyper. That's the worst part, being teased with a glimpse of those ships, reminded of all the things out there I'll never, *ever*, see. All the things I'm missing.'

Sean knew what she meant. Most of the farm kids living on isolated farm plots like theirs seemed to be content with their lot, but he, like Ellie, wanted to see more.

'Listen Ellie, I'm not telling anyone, okay? I promise.'

She nodded gratefully.

'But I've got to say something. Running away over there,' he gestured in the direction of New Haven, 'is going to be a hard deal. Life is harsh and expensive. I've been there a few times with my Dad. If you've got money, yeah, it's a playground. But if you don't...well, it can be rough. There's all sorts living there, non-humans, off-worlders. There're a lot of bad areas, a lot of people who will happily take advantage of you, rip you off.'

'I know it'll be hard at first. But I can't *not* do it.' She looked at him. 'Does that make sense?'

He nodded gently. Of course it made sense. But he was worried that Ellie would walk into New Haven looking like the perfect target for every lowlife there. She was young for nineteen; looked young, behaved young. Add to that the instantly recognizable hick-naivety of some poor soil-scratcher from out of town looking to find her fortune. She'd be a walking target.

'I know you've probably thought a lot about this, and think you've thought this all through and have some kind of perfect plan to get yourself sorted out quickly and-'

'At least I've got to try.'

'Sure, but maybe if you were to talk this through with your Mum and Dad, they'll be able to help you.'

'They'll just try to talk me out of it Sean. You know that.'

'Uh-huh. Of course they will. They at least deserve the chance to do that. Your Mum and Dad, they're good people Ellie…they love you.'

'I know, but don't you think I've considered everything you've said just now? Crudge, I can see how my cruddy life goes…staying on here farming indefinitely and watching everyone else my age disappear off to the city or even leaving this world. And me, slowly growing old, alone in my own three-square- acre universe. If I don't go soon I'll find myself getting sucked into running Dad's farm, and then I'll never get the chance!'

He knew there was nothing he could say in response to that. Because she was quite right.

'Please don't tell them,' she asked.

An awkward silence.

'I'd better head back home, it's getting late.'

'Promise me you won't tell anyone,' Ellie pleaded.

'I told you. I promise,' Sean replied solemnly. 'I'll let myself out.'

He headed towards the entrance to the domestic area then found himself turning back to look at her. Ellie was gazing up again at the stars.

'How much chore money have you managed to save?' he whispered.

'Three hundred and fifty-six creds.'

He winced. He guessed that was enough money to rent a room in the city for a couple of weeks, a seedy one at that. He could see a disturbing range of future scenarios ahead for her, the best-case one being her returning to this farm, her dreams of escape in tatters, broken-hearted and penniless.

'I'll see you same time next week; remember to bone up on that dom-tech module.'

Ellie didn't reply. He thought that maybe she was crying.

OMNIPEDIA:
[Human Universe: digital encyclopedia]

Article: Harpers Reach - The birth planet of Ellie Quin'

Harpers Reach was a planet in the Seventh Veil that was first charted and surveyed in 3041, seventy years after the Colonial Wars had come to an end. As a consequence, this new frontier planet had never, mercifully, experienced first-hand - unlike established worlds caught up in that conflict - the horrors of post-fusion warfare. It was, however, a planet on the very edge of Human Space, away from the densest trade routes and the prosperity that that brings. It was also woefully short of valuable, tradable natural resources that might have attracted commerce towards it. It's only merit was that it offered a sizeable surface of seismically stable real estate.

Harpers Reach was always destined to be a poor, under-achieving, uninteresting frontier world. Doomed, like most of its inhabitants, to irrelevance from birth.

At the time of Ellie Quin's childhood, Harpers Reach was in the middle of an extended economic recession. It was a planet that was still too young to have matured out of its two domed cities to establish extensive industry across the planet's surface. In addition, the principal city, *New Haven*, a sprawling and squalid metropolis, was becoming swollen with ecological migrants from the nearby failed colony world of *Celestion*.

User Comment > SpingleBrick
I herd Harpers Reach wuz never real. Itz all mad up conspirisy by the govvyment cuz they like to make liez an stuff.

User Comment > BiiiiiG-Boy
Helloooo gentlemens! Is your sex drive failing you? Do you wish you could make love all night long like a true God!? Then try *CosmoRod Stim-Shakers*. Three strokes and your partner will be in seventh heaven!

User Comment > Anonymous
To the complete ditto-head above - Harpers Reach is real. And it's still there you idiot. They do archaeological tours there. Look it

up. (Why do all the stupidest people in the universe have to post here on Omnipedia? There's plenty of other places uniweb for you vegetables to gather.)

User Comment > XXX-come-buy-XXX
want to buy black market alien sex tapes?

CHAPTER 4

Dr Edward Mason stared out of the window of his dark study, down at the azure panorama below. He loved this view. It would be the one thing he truly missed.

He turned his back on the blue vista of Pacifica, the ocean world, above which the labs hung in static orbit. There were things to be done. He was due on the mid-morning shuttle down to Pacifica, to all intents and purposes to embark on a long overdue two week sailing vacation, away from his work. But in actual fact Mason was quietly preparing to disappear for good; to leave behind his tiresome, largely managerial, role here at the Department of Genetic Analysis.

For thirty years Mason had been in charge of the enormous cluster of laboratories floating above Pacifica; three decades running the department for the Administration. And in that time, dutifully doing his job, overseeing his staff as they collated genetic data from the *millions* of paternity requests that flooded in from all corners of Human Space. Playing God;

deciding which hopeful citizens would be granted permission to have children, and which would be denied.

Mason recalled the line from a popular song from a few years ago: *it's was all down to them genes, groovy-oovy genes, bay-beee!!*

Playing with our genes – vetting, approving, editing, rewriting precious passages of genetic data for convenience, to suit central government's - the Administration's - needs.

Oh yes, the department did a hell of a lot more than just collating the DNA of eager parents to-be. The ready-to-grow embryos that Mason's department returned to those hopeful parents around the universe were *mostly* the product of their blood – with a few tweaks added for good measure.

Meddling, *enhancing*, along guidelines provided to Mason from the Administration. Small things of course; enhanced bone structure for embryos due to be returned to hi-gravity worlds, UV-resistant skin pigments for those returning to weak-atmosphere worlds. But also subtle behavioral adjustments to ensure these precious little embryos grew up to be reliable, compliant little citizens.

It had been like this since natural fertility had been bred out for practical reasons, many hundreds of years ago, each new generation was grown to order now. Each new generation tinkered with.

Mason sat down at his mock-mahogany desk and continued the task he had been working on all morning. He waved his hand over the desk sensor and his holo-screen display flickered on before him. His personal data space was full of essays and notes he had written during his long tenure here, essays that had grown more hectoring and worrisome in tone as the years had passed. Essays high-lighting the growing occurrence of serious congenital disorders, mutations. Little by little, the inevitable genetic errors, an unavoidable result of so much *editing*, were mounting up. And Mason was seeing the laboratories producing more and more freaks in-vitro with each passing week.

They were destroying the human genome.

Mason had long ago given up sending these essays of concern back to the Administration. He knew there was little they would do even if they wanted to. Population distribution within Human Space *needed* to be tightly managed. There were too many fragile young worlds in early phases of terra-forming that could barely sustain their small populations. The paternity requests approved to those places *had* to be only for children of healthy, hardy parents who contributed in some way to that process. And even then, they needed tweaking to be that bit more healthy and productive than their parents.

Tough life forging some remote colony on a far-flung world. Any little extra help; firmer bones, thicker UV-resistant skin was a good thing.

And let's not forget, deciding who shall have children and who shan't is a very useful chokehold. Rebellious planet? Not a problem, just don't let 'em breed. They'll die out soon enough.

Mason suspected that the bureaucrats of the Administration were all too aware that every year the mutation levels were getting worse. But they had no choice, not if they wanted to hold on to the way things were. This system worked for them. For better or for worse.

Mason dragged his notes, his essays, his digital scribblings across to the DELETE icon in the corner of his workspace, then had second thoughts. Deleted files were compressed and kept in a central 'pending' archive, sometimes for several weeks before being automatically wiped. They could be easily retrieved before that happened. And read. He couldn't afford for that to happen.

Oh, if only delete actually meant delete.

Instead he dragged all of the collected files into an obscure data folder, one protected by a password and innocuously named 'Stats-Temp'. He knew his assistant, Rowan Brown would dutifully and respectfully clear out his old files, purging all of his personal data space after he'd spent all of five minutes mourning his boss's death. Brown so-o-o wanted this office cubicle, this desk, this view and wouldn't wait to get started making this space his own.

Mason dropped the files into the directory and nodded with satisfaction. Brown would erase it. And that was fine. Just as long as there was nothing lying around related to file L-239-HR-2457709. Nothing at all…that would lead anyone to that child.

He smiled.

L-239-HR-2457709. She would be approaching twenty years of age by now. Emotions would be stirring within her, the desire to spread her wings and fly overpowering. He wondered what she looked like, what her parents had named her. Above all else, Mason wished he knew that – what her name was. He had the surname of course – Quin. And the citizen ID numbers for L-239's parents - enough information to locate the family easily enough. He had those two crucial little items of information written by hand in his personal note book. That was the beauty of his old fountain pen and paper, there was no digital trail left behind them.

He closed down the data terminal and the holo-screen vanished.

It was time to go find her and watch over her; to look out for her. She was more precious than *anything* else in the universe, so incredibly precious. Mason allowed himself to think of L-239 as *his* child. In a way she was as much his. Twenty years ago he had selected one particular paternity request out of the millions. The gene-stock was good, the family well away out of harm's way, anonymous and healthy folk, perfect. And with great care he had authored this creature to be the very beginning of the end…of the way things are.

If the Administration knew she was out there, if they knew something this dangerous to them, to all they held dear, was somewhere out there, they would destroy entire star systems to get their hands on her.

To kill her.

Mason patted his jacket and felt the subtle form of his notebook nestling snugly in his inside pocket. He looked once more around his desk and his cluttered study. If there was anything at all incriminating left behind, something that he had somehow overlooked then at worst he'd be leaving behind evidence on non-approved genetic work. The only possible information that could lead them to her…was what was written by hand and sitting in his pocket.

Good. Then it was time for Dr Edward Mason to go and 'die'.

CHAPTER 5

The central dome of the Quin farm was roughly half a square acre of rubbertex-covered ground. It was filled with a scruffy looking arrangement of several habi-cubes; the prefabricated alloy cabins that were an ever present eye-sore on any hard-scrabble colony world. They arranged in an approximate circle around an open middle, a space the family liked to call the *courtyard*. It was an apt name for this patch of ground beneath the apex of the central dome, with a matt of plastic brush that was meant to be 'grass' and a selection of large potted plants, some of which were actually real. It had the vague feel of a cloistered garden. Or that was the point anyway.

The courtyard had, by default, become the 'flop out' zone for the Quins, and was littered with deck chairs, Ted's lazily discarded toys, a number of Dad's Jacob's half-finished furniture repair jobs and a family sized hammock strung between two dome support rods painted and tricked-out to look a bit like palm trees trunks.

On the toob they were watching a documentary on the ecological disaster that happened on Celestion a few years ago. Today, in fact, was the seventh anniversary of that horrific event. It was a program on the toob that Dad particularly wanted to see, announcing that fact this morning over breakfast. Ted had predictably whined when the set had been turned from the toon channel, but he'd given up pretty quickly. There was an unspoken protocol within the home that if Dad wanted to watch something on the toob, then Dad got to watch it. From the first mewling cry of frustration Ted had known the exercise was futile. He'd stormed off to his habi-cube stamping his feet heavily.

The rest of them sat in the comfort of the courtyard. Mum had brought out dinner, set it down on several unfolding plastic tables and dimmed the lights; the only illumination being the flickering glow of the holo-toob itself.

Ellie remembered watching the tragic event unfold *live* on the toob seven years ago. She had only been twelve back then. Old enough to fully understand what was happening on the nearby planet. The whole universe must have tuned in to watch the news as every available surface vessel on the planet converged on Casares - the planet's one, doomed city - to try and evacuate as many of the denizens there as time would allow. As it happened only a few thousand managed to get out before a tsunami of truly apocalyptic proportions slammed into the fragile city.

Amongst the city's trapped population, a news team had been down there and they'd filmed the phenomenon as it raced towards the city. Its horrendous approach was described by news anchor Henry Marlett, a well-groomed middle-aged man Ellie recalled had at one time been a regular newsreader on Harpers Reach. She remembered being chilled to the bone by the sight of what appeared to be a mountain range on the move. It was as it drew closer and rose high enough to brush the base clouds in the sky that she realized it was a tidal wave. The cool matter-of-factness of Marlett's narrative as the final moment arrived had stuck in her mind all these years.

She remembered thinking how bizarre it was that anyone could remain so calm with something like that bearing down on them.

How a person could even manage to string a sentence together, or operate a camera, or carry on holding a boom mic while knowing they were only seconds away from a violent end. The Quins watched in silence as the oft-aired and all too familiar minute-long sequence played out the awful drama once again. No matter how many times Ellie saw this piece of film, it still managed to make the hairs on her forearms rise and her skin to goose bump like a chicken drumstick.

'It's now...it must be a mile away...but its moving fast. You can see from these pictures that the height of this wave must be nearly a thousand feet...'

A dark undulating horizon, featureless at this distance, slowly rises menacingly. In the background can be heard many different, tense voices. This must have been the news production team, kept from the very cusp of panic by having the important job of documenting their own deaths.

'It's quite awe-inspiring. There is no doubt now that this wave will completely engulf Casares. There had been a hope that the energy of the would have been reduced by the time it reached us here, but clearly

this is a wave that will leave no building standing and probably no-one alive...'

The sound of somebody crying. Too much now for one of Marlett's team.

'It looks like it's about half a mile from me now...maybe even closer. I can see some surface vessels, shuttles, and boats even, caught in its grasp. They're turning over and over, rolling down the front face of the wave like discarded toys. My god...this is an incredible and terrifying sight.'

The image is beginning to wobble. Marlett looks at someone off screen...the cameraman? He mouths 'you want me to take it?' A moment later the camera changes hands and Marlett is now holding it. From now on only he can be heard.

'The wave is now, I guess, less than a quarter of a mile away. We only have a few seconds left until it hits us. When it does, the building I am standing in will simply cease to exist, everyone here will die more or less instantly. The camera may survive a little longer and successfully transmit images to you. I am placing the camera on a table...'

The image pans wildly and then it is perfectly still and facing a broad bay window looking out on to the metallic-

colored water of a shallow cove and the churning wall of black water beyond. There is no longer a sky, just a wall of water. Marlett appears in the shot again a few moments later beside the bay window. He places his arms protectively around the shoulders of a couple of younger people. A fatherly gesture for his loyal broadcast team. Together they stare out at the approaching wall. In the final second before the wall hits, Marlett turns back to the camera and smiles. A goodbye to someone close.

In an instant the image is mottled with white frothing water. It lasts only two seconds before transmissions ceases.

Ellie shuddered.

'Cool,' said Ted enthusiastically.

Ellie and her parents turned towards him.

'I thought you were meant to be sulking in your bedroom dipweed?' snapped Ellie.

'I was, dogface,' he said irritatingly, flicking his wrist to click his fingers.

Shona sniggered.

'That,' said Ellie pointing towards the toob, still emotionally charged by the clip, 'was not cool you simpleton dwarf boy. It was horrific.'

'Nah, it was triple cool. Imagine surfing that monster wave…'

Dad stepped in, 'Ted…you should know better. It wasn't a cartoon. A lot of people died when that happened. Normal folk, just like us. Would that be cool? A huge tidal wave wiping us away?'

Ted shook his head sheepishly.

'Right. So I don't want to hear 'cool' right now.'

Ted pouted under his father's withering gaze, but once Jacob Quin turned back to continue watching the toob Ted discreetly stuck his tongue out at Ellie.

'Ted, stop winding up you sister,' said Maria spotting his sly gesture.

Ellie smiled. *Mum: Queen of Peripheral Vision*.

Ted headed back to his cabin pretending to surf when his parents were not looking.

Ellie shook her head. 'He's such an idiot…are you sure we're related Mum?'

Maria smiled. 'Oh, we found him in the recycling bin as a baby. He looked far too pitiful to throw away. So we kept him.'

CHAPTER 6

They were at the Traders' Show.

The Traders' Show was where the farmers in the region went to buy equipment and haggle over the next season's crop prices with the distribution and shipping agents. It was a big deal for the local farming community and it happened once a year. The whole thing had started out twenty-three years ago as a simple rendezvous arranged between a dozen farmers and the only agent from New Haven who was prepared to travel out of town and deal with them. Over the years the rendezvous had grown and attracted other agents, wholesalers and distributors as well as the usual motley assortment of traders and dealers, importers and exporters, trinket sellers, fast food stalls, travelling salesmen, side shows, fair rides and con men. It had snowballed rapidly over the last seven years according to Jacob and now, with all the things there were to see and do, it was almost inexcusable for a farmer to turn up and leave his family behind.

Originally, the event had taken place in a shuttle station sixty miles west of the Quin's farm. But it soon outgrew this venue and now was housed in a large, twenty-acre plexitex dome beside the station.

It was the One Big Thing that the spread-out and isolated farming families in the area looked forward to all year; a chance for everyone to scrub up and put on their best clothes and step out. But for Ellie, it felt like getting a whiff of the big city; a try-before-you-buy sampler of what it might be like in New Haven.

She loved it.

Ellie and Shona were taking their time deciding how to spend the five creds Dad had given each of them that morning. He called it 'fun money', actually it was more like leave-me-alone money.

Jacob Quin was going to be spending the entire day down at the exchange, mostly haggling next season oxygen-crop prices with his current agent. But Ellie also knew that the day would be spent shooting the breeze with other farmers, acquaintances, friends and possibly - no probably - sinking a few beers.

Shona was humming and clucking over whether to splash the lot in a single moment of consumer madness; to indulge in the mindless pleasure of a spending orgy on a variety of trinkets and baubles or purchase a single plastic jacket with a counterfeit off-world designer logo on it she had spotted on a stall nearby. The desire to own one of these over-priced, poorly mass-manufactured designer garments was eating her up inside.

Ellie spotted some Crazie-Beanie merchandise. Crazie-Beanie was an amusing high-pitched warbling voice-over for an anti-bacterial wipe advert. The voice and the catch-phrase had caught on over the last year. And, of course, now a little character existed to go along with it. Despite the fact it was a kids thing, Ellie loved Crazie-Beanie. The trilling, gibbering nonsense he spouted during the advert for anti-bacterial wipes, and the other dozen or so products he now endorsed, made her giggle. She was browsing through some Beanie-bangles when she heard a voice.

'Hi Ellie, hey Shon'…how are you guys enjoying the show?' It was Sean.

Shona flushed self-consciously looking down at her shuffling feet in a futile attempt to hide her crimson cheeks.

'It's alright, same as last year and the year before that…and so on,' said Ellie casually, she hoped. 'Same guff, different year.'

He smiled, 'I guess you've seen one, you've seen them all.'

'Something like that. You here with your Dad?'

'Yup, he's probably the same place as yours right now, haggling with the agents.'

'Or trying to persuade my Dad to change over the crop again.'

'Makes sense though, Ellie. Every year the atmosphere grows a little more O-rich, that can't be doing your Dad a favor when it comes to negotiating the best sell price.'

Sean, of course, was right. Although the last few years had seen an influx of off-worlders to New Haven which had driven up demand for O2 supplies to the two domed cities, the trend was definitely a downward one. Ten or twenty years from now the price of oxygen per canister would be half its value.

'The word amongst the agents is *meat crops*. Or so I've been told,' he added.

Ellie curled her lip in disgust. They had once tried growing a small plot of these some years back as an experiment. The heat in the bio-dome had been too much and the entire batch had died and gone off overnight. In death, the plants derma-husks had ruptured spilling offal and a bloody, rancid soup over the floor of the dome. The Quin family woke up the next morning to find the dome resembled an abattoir.

Sean turned to Shona and handed her some creds. 'Listen Shona, can you do me a favor?'

She nodded enthusiastically, 'sure.'

'Can you buy us some fagurters? No sauce for me... and anything you want for yourself, okay?'

Shona was thrilled to have some bonus creds to spend and was immediately gone, pushing through the milling crowd of people towards the nearest food vendor. Sean waited until he saw her join a queue before he began.

'I wanted to talk to you Ellie, alone.'

Ellie felt her skin prickle in anticipation. She guessed he was about to say something that was going to make her feel utterly shitty and hate him. Given their last conversation, she fully expected him to confess that he'd told her Dad about her plans to run away to New Haven.

'I've thought about last week-'

Here it comes, thanks Sean, thank you so very fregging much.

Ellie turned to him. 'So?'

'So...I've decided that if you insist on running away to New Haven, then maybe I'll help you out. I'll take you there myself.'

Ellie stared in silence at him, unsure whether he was serious or not.

'Ellie? You okay?'

She swayed slightly, feeling light headed, 'you...you're serious? You'll go with me?'

Sean nodded.

'Go with me? You mean...*stay* with me?' A rush of fantasies momentarily filled her head; the pair of them, together, *an item*, in New Haven. She closed her eyes and saw a fleeting image of them together locked in a passionate embrace on the balcony of some luxurious apartment overlooking the most spectacular cityscape imaginable. A forest of glistening metal and glass structures descending into a bustling urban carpet beneath them, and the sky around them buzzing with sky-cars and shuttles, the whole scene bathed in a rich golden sunset. In her mind's eye, she felt the firm, taut body of Sean pressed against her, his strong arms enveloping her and protecting her from the world outside like a force field. She felt his soft lips against hers and stroked his delicious jaw as they kissed, feeling the gentle rasp of his closely shaved skin…

'I don't mean I'm going to stay.'

Pop. That little fantasy bubble burst too easily.

'Listen Ellie, I'll take you to New Haven with me a few weeks ahead of the Freezer's scheduled arrival, so I can help you find a place, get a job…you know, get started. Okay?'

'You…you're still going off-world then?

'Yeah, I'm still going. But you should be settled in by the time I leave, maybe found some work, someplace to live and-'

'But…but won't we be living together in our own place? For a few weeks? Living together…just like…just like-'

'As *friends,* Ellie, that's all. Good, close friends. No more than that, and just for a few weeks.'

She steadied her voice. Conjured up a dismissive grin. 'Yeah, that's what I meant. Buddies. Best buddies. I…'

Sean cupped her chin in his hand, he couldn't help but see the momentary twinkle of a suppressed tear in the flickering side-show carnival lights.

'I'm not a complete idiot. I know how you feel.' He struggled to find the right blend of words. 'If things were different. If I wasn't going…maybe you and I…?'

'We'd eventually get together?'

He nodded an answer rather than actually saying it. Well, not so much nodded, as shrugged. But it was an affirmation of sorts.

'Sean…'

Oh, don't say it, Ellie. Really. Don't say it.

'Sean, I really…'

Don't be a complete fregging moron. What she wanted to say - *needed* to say - felt like wind; halfway up and determined to burp out of her mouth. 'Sean, I think I love you.'

Idiot! Idiot! Idiot! Id- Errrr…hang on, did he actually just wince?

'Look, Ellie, I'm very fond of you too.'

And there, he just said 'fond'.

In summary; you idiot. She felt her face flush. She'd always thought there was a ghost of a chance there. That perhaps if one evening during a math class, if she made a rash move on him. Perhaps a jokey play-wrestle that somehow randomly – deliberately - ended up with him pinned down and their faces inches apart...the rest would just kind of happen.

'Ellie, I...this is uh, a bit awkward. It's not that I don't-'

'I'm plain. That's it? Plain and dull.'

'No! God, no! It's not that.' Sean shook his head. He looked up to see where Shona was. She was still queuing to be served. 'It's just...I just...'

'What?'

Sean pressed his lips. 'You're kind of what I'm running away from.'

Ellie felt like he'd just punched her in the ribs.

'No, see, that came out sounding all wrong. You *represent* it. No. What I mean is...Harpers Reach, this world. Farm-fregging-life. I hate it. It's suffocating. I want what's way out there, beyond the sky. I want that!'

'And I'm just a part of this dull ol' life?'

He stopped a nod. 'Yes, but. You're the only interesting part of it, Ellie. That's my point. You want the same as me. Maybe even want it more than me. If there was any fairness in the universe it would be you going, not me.' Sean shook his head. 'I'm not making much sense, am I?'

'Oh, I get it.' She nodded. 'You want to leave this all behind you. No strings. A new shiny life.' She dabbed at her face. Damned if she was going to let him see a tear rolling down her cheek. 'I guess I'd be the same if it was me.'

'But I don't want to go and be worrying about you, Ellie. I want to go knowing you're going to be all right.'

'Why worry? You'll be gone. A new life an' all that.'

'Because maybe after my eight years tour of duty I want to know there's someone special to come home to?'

Shit! He's asking me to wait for him? She was halfway between gushing with rekindled hope, and decking him for being so fregging arrogant. Oh yeah, Sean wanted to see the universe; to fight and shag his way around the planets of Human Space, and then know he could come home to Loyal Little Ellie Quin. Waiting patiently for him?

Tell him to go freg himself. Ellie. Tell him to-

She smiled. 'I'd like that.'

Idiot!

She told her brain to shut up. And added for good measure, that maybe, just maybe, she'd make sure they had at least one long night together before he went. Confirmation that she was more than a dumb math student and a friend. So much more than a kid now.

A woman.

He looked up to see where Shona was again. 'Listen, if you really want to go to New Haven then I think we should leave soon. My Dad's given me a load of creds. He wants me to go see the city before I leave, have a ball, y'know? Live a little before the marines get their hands on me. So I can leave any time now. I've got the money to find us somewhere half-decent to rent whilst we get you sorted out.'

Ellie felt a surge of excitement as she listened to Sean thinking aloud. 'Also,' Sean continued, 'Dad has a couple of friends in the city, we can maybe look them up, see if they can help you out with a job.'

'You'd do all this for me?'

'I'm doing it because I know you'd go and do this on your own anyway.'

Ellie shrugged nonchalantly and nodded. He wasn't wrong.

'And if you walk into New Haven with just three hundred creds and no return ticket home you're going to end up in big trouble. At least this way, when I leave I'll know you're okay and not walking the streets. But I'm doing this on one condition.'

'What?'

'When we go, you leave a letter for your Mum and Dad. And when I leave Harpers Reach you make sure you stay in touch with them. Okay?'

'Okay.'

Shona was getting served now. She would be back in a minute.

'We'll talk about this some more when I come over next week for your studies. But like I say, we should go sooner rather than later. The more time we have in the city before I have to leave on the Freezer, the better.'

Ellie nodded silently. She could see Shona beginning to weave her way back through the crowd towards them. Before her sister got too close Ellie decided to kiss him on the cheek. He didn't flinch. There was no awkwardness or passion in it, just warmth and gratitude. 'Thank you,' she said in a whisper, 'for doing this for me.'

Sean stared at her firmly. There was something about this girl, something that set her apart from the other farm kids he knew and the few city people he'd met. Her eyes always seemed focused on the far away things; horizons, star ships, distant cities. He knew she was going to run to the city with or without his help. He suspected there was an iron-rod of will inside Ellie that perhaps one day would be the making of her, or perhaps the end of her.

'I know you're meant for something better than this. I can see it, *feel* it. Call it a hunch, but someday not only will you outgrow New Haven, you'll make it off-world too.'

She shrugged, 'I'd love to think so.'

They both heard Shona whistling a jingle as she approached them with a carrier bag full of steaming, savory treats.

'Umm…you guys look busy, you want me to leave again?' she asked with a mischievous grin.

Sean broke his gaze from Ellie and cracked a smile for Shona. 'No need, just giving your sister a pep talk, she needs to put a little more work into her math.'

'Uh-huh, didn't look like that to me,' she said with a knowing wink.

CHAPTER 7

'...So you see, it's really happening Hufty. I'm going at last.'

Ellie snapped off the mic' of her diary. She gazed at the shimmering horizon - the humidity was low enough this morning to catch the distant reflective glint of sunlight on the dome over New Haven. From her favorite perch-point up here on the overlook she could see horizon three-sixty degrees around her. The terrain was a relentless rust red, broken with occasional patches of ochre, the hardy native lichen of this planet and, in fact, pretty much the only form of indigenous life discovered on Harpers Reach.

Down below she could see her Dad carrying out some routine maintenance on one of the domes. From this distance it was hard to see what he was up to, but Ellie guessed he was repairing wear-and-tear holes in the plexitex. The business of growing an oxygen crop was hard enough work without losing the valuable profit to rips in the plastic skin. She watched him stand up, arch his back and tiredly wipe his brow.

It was thirsty work, standing out here in the mercilessly intense glare of the sun. A job Jacob Quin wished he could afford to have subcontracted to some maintenance company. Not being able to afford such a luxury meant it was an endless chore he had to do himself, or lose money through seepage.

He was constantly reminded of how the perceived value of oxygen was slowly sliding. Not just the gentle but persistent decline in price over recent years, but in other ways too. Twenty years ago when he had started out, the O2 industry planet-wide had been treated with respect. Whether you were a small independent farmer, or a worker in a large refinery or even just a buying-agent, association to this life-sustaining resource had a noticeable effect on the way people treated you. It was respect, but it came across almost as gratitude, despite the fact that everyone in the oxygen business was in it for hard profit, not out of some altruistic sense of civic duty. Nowadays, of course, as testing stations around the world were starting to register pockets of atmosphere with nearly tolerable levels of O2 on a regular basis, courtesy of the Oxxon refineries in the north pole, the business was starting to lose its kudos. In the not too distant future it would lose its ability to make money.

It was finally time, he decided, to move over to something new.

He studied the plastic patch he had just applied to a jagged rip in the dome.

At least when the air on Harpers Reach becomes rich enough to put the likes of me out of business there'll be no need for these damn domes any more.

He heard Ellie approach. The clattering of pebbles and small rocks tumbling down the slope gave her away long before she slapped her hand amicably on his sweaty shoulder.

'You missed a bit,' she laughed, her voice sounded muffled through the oxygen mask.

'Oh, spectacularly funny. You come to give me a hand?'

'Why not.'

Jacob Quin looked curiously at his daughter. 'Okay, what are you after?' he asked with a tone of suspicion.

'Nothing. I just guess it's about time I gave you a hand with this particularly shitty job.'

'Better late than never, I suppose. Oh, and less of the 'shitty'. Your mother hears potty-mouth like that and it's me that's going to get it, not you.'

'Freggin' sorry 'bout that.'

Jacob smirked, 'Thadda-girl. Anyway, you've got to hold something back for a stubbed toe.'

Ellie studied her father work as he resumed the process of patching up the plexitex. Around the base of all three domes occurred the worst wear and tear. The occasional strong winds would scoop up clouds of dust and gravel that would scour, wear thin and occasionally tear the plastic sheath. Larger items of wind-borne debris would simply punch a hole through. Jacob routinely and laboriously checked the entire perimeter of his farm each and every week, often finding dozens of tattered holes to repair. Ellie squatted down beside her father as he finished off applying and sealing a patch with the plasti-welder.

'You want to have a go?' he asked.

'Sure.'

He passed it to her. It looked like a soldering iron. 'Just run it slowly along the edge of the patch. Don't stop…just keep moving or you'll melt right through and then we'll have to patch the patch.'

Ellie applied the welder along the remaining seam. The plastic sizzled and bonded instantly.

He rapped the patch with his knuckles. 'Good as new. See? Easy, huh?'

'And strangely fun.'

'Great. I'll get us another welder for your birthday then.'

Ellie laughed, 'okay, to be clear…not *that* much fun.'

He stood up. 'Come on. More holes to fill.'

The pair of them walked slowly, scanning the base of Booster and periodically stopping to stick on a patch. A good half-hour passed in silence as they slowly broiled in the hot morning sun.

'We're going to be okay, aren't we Dad?' Ellie asked suddenly as she wiped a bead of sweat from her brow.

'Okay? What are you talking about?'

'The future, the way things are heading in the long run. I just want to know that things will be okay.'

Jacob turned to Ellie, 'has someone been feeding you scare stories?'

Ellie didn't answer.

'Let me guess…Sean?.

Ellie nodded reluctantly.

'Well don't worry about letting on and dropping him in it. His father gave me the same lecture as Sean has given you, I'm sure.'

'And?' she asked.

'And…it's annoying having everyone tell you how to run your agri-plot. But to answer your question though, things are going to be fine in the long-run. I'm going to think about trying a meat crop again.'

Ellie smiled and gave him a thumbs-up.

'But, if we do go ahead and change the crop,' he continued, 'it's going to cost us a fair bit to adjust. We'll need to tighten our belts over the next few years.'

Ellie slapped him proudly on the back. 'Well done Dad. I know how hard a decision that was for you.'

Jacob Quin shook his head sadly. 'I've been an oxygen man since before you were born. I guess we all knew the business wouldn't last forever.'

'That's right. We've done well out of tubweed, haven't we? I mean, you own the farm, we have a home, we're not in debt. Things are fine aren't they Dad?'

'Yup, things are fine. I guess it's just that after all these years of learning how to grow the stupid things, rigging the domes to just the right temperature and moisture, you know? Getting It Right. And now I've got to start over.'

Ellie knew how stubborn her father was, how difficult it was for him to adjust when needs required it. In her mind's eye she had seen her father farming tubweed to the end of his days and steering them all inexorably towards bankruptcy and a tough life of subsistence and making do. Since talking to Sean at the fair she'd nursed a residual concern about leaving them for New Haven; a worry that the family business would soon begin to be affected by the distant, as yet, but inevitable, O2 industry recession.

'So anyway, why are you so interested all of a sudden? Not that I mind you showing an interest.'

Ellie shrugged, 'I just wanted to be sure things're going to be alright.'

'Why? You going someplace?'

She froze. She looked at him. He was being flippant. 'Nah…just watching out for my inheritance.'

Jacob winked at her. 'Good girl.' He reached out and ruffled her hair. She went through a stage of hating gestures like that; being treated like a son, a tom-boy. A favorite farm hand. But right now she relished it; this one last moment of connection with Dad. Savored it and knew there'd be a time soon enough that she'd miss it.

'We'll be fine Ellie.'

She smiled. 'I know.'

The pair of them finished the weekly inspection tour half an hour later and went in gasping for something ice-cold to drink. Jacob split a can of beer with her without a second thought and despite disliking its metallic taste, she proudly chugged it down in several manly gulps.

CHAPTER 8

Ted had the habit of sleepwalking around the central dome in just his underwear. It bugged the hell out of Ellie, particularly when he decided to amble into her cabin unannounced.

'Shit! Hey, Ted!…ever heard of knocking?' she said snapping off her diary and throwing a sweatshirt over her narrow shoulders.

Ted swayed sleepily in the doorway, his hair tousled and fluffed up on one side like a hairy horn. His cheeks were flushed and judging by the look of his sleepy and teary face, he had been having a bad dream.

'Ellie…where've they taken my Baxter?…he's gone.'

Ted had had an android pet, a puppy dog. For most kids needing an android pet was usually a short-lived phase experienced between the ages of three and six. It was little more than a fad that most kids grew out of in the space of a year. Ted had grown unhealthily close to his and Mum and Dad had taken it away from him not many months after his sixth birthday; they had begun to worry about his excessive attachment to what was really nothing more than a simple circuit board covered in fur. For Ted the whole incident had proved to be quite traumatic and even now, just over a year later, he still occasionally awoke in the middle of the night and reached out for his beloved dog for a reassuring cuddle. On those occasions he usually ended up tearfully and sleepily walking across the courtyard to Ellie's cabin.

Her irritation evaporated when she realized that this would probably be the last time she would be carrying her little brother back to bed. He wasn't so bad, as far as little dwarf boy brothers went.

She got up from her desk, walked over to the doorway and knelt down beside him.

'He's gone Ted, gone away to doggy heaven. Come on little guy, let's get you back to bed.'

She turned her back towards him and he automatically hung his arms around her neck and climbed aboard, still more asleep than awake. Ellie stood up carrying him piggy-back and stepped out of her habi-cube. Ted stirred as she walked lightly across the 'grass', the plastic fibres rustling noisily against her bare feet.

'Don't put me back in bed…please?'

She had things to do.

'You're not a dogface. In fact, you're prettier than Shona,' he said.

The little rascal, she thought. He could charm the birds from the trees, if there'd been birds or trees. She clucked and hummed, feigning indecision.

'Ple-e-ea-se, Ellie?'

'Okay, but just five minutes, then I'm putting you back in your bed. You want to sit out here for a while?'

Ted nodded. Ellie walked over to the hammock, tipped him gently in and clambered on beside him. The hammock swung slowly causing the support poles to creak rhythmically. Ellie stared up at the rich purple night sky through the clear plastic of the dome. Ted followed her gaze.

'I like stars…I wish we had a spaceship,' he said, more thinking aloud than talking to Ellie.

'So do I,' she agreed.

'If you had a spaceship, where would you go?'

Ellie looked at Ted. That seemed to be a curious question for him to be posing. 'Why are you asking me that?'

'I dunno...just asking. Me, I'd go to Danger Nebula 5.'

'Ted, that's just a pretend place.'

'It's where the Plasma Rangers base is,' he replied indignantly.

Ellie sighed. Ted was proof that too much lazing around in front of the kids channel turned you into an idiot. 'The Plasma Rangers is a cartoon my dear little brother. Therefore, it is not real life and they do not exist.'

Ted sat up, 'I know, I'm not a baby.'

Ellie goosed his neck. 'No, I guess you're not anymore.'

He lay back down in the hammock, satisfied with getting that admission out of her. 'So where would *you* go?'

'Anywhere but here,' she said a little too quickly. She hoped Ted had missed that. He said nothing. For a while they lay in silence, swinging gently and listening to the creak of the poles.

In the sky above, a distant transport ship entered the upper ionosphere with a flicker of blue light and slowly moved across the golden misty slash of the Seventh Veil towards the south.

From the smooth rustle of his breathing, she thought Ted had already fallen asleep. But he spoke quietly. 'Are you going to leave home?'

Ellie lay in stunned silence. It seemed like the whole world was able to guess her business. 'What?! Of course not. What gave…'

'You're not? Oh, well you should do. I am. As soon as I'm growed up, I'm going to be a pulse warrior. They live on the planet Pulsator.'

Ellie relaxed. 'Ted, has anyone ever told you you're a toon addict?'

'Yup. Mum does every day.'

Ellie dug her thumbs into his ribs and Ted squirmed in the hammock like a fish in a net. Something else she realized she actually might end up missing; the rough and tumble fun with the little couch potato.

'Come on monkey boy, time's up. Let's get you back to bed.'

*

The next day Sean arrived on time for Ellie's weekly math session. He pulled up outside the Quin farm in his father's dirt-cat amidst a cloud of red dust. Maria watched him from the entrance hatchway as he climbed out and hastily jogged towards her, not bothering with an O2 mask. She swung open the hatch as he arrived and quickly closed it once he was inside.

'You really ought to have a mask with you all the time Sean, just to be safe. I might not have been at the door ready to open it.'

He smiled patiently at Mrs Quin. She was the over-cautious, wrap-'em-up-in-cotton-wool-until-they-suffocate type.

'How are your folks?' she asked.

'Fine, Mrs Quin.'

'Jeez, you can call me Maria if you want. You've been coming here for years…I would have thought we'd be past the 'Mrs Quin' stage by now.'

'Sorry, it's habit.'

'Hmm, not long now is it, the marine ship? I bet you're excited?'

'Yes ma'am, two months. I can't wait.'

Maria called out Ellie's name. There was no answer. 'I guess she'll be outside up on her perch.'

'I'll drive up. See you later, Mrs Quin.' He opened the hatch and ran across the open clay to the dirt-cat. Maria again hastily closed the hatch, begrudging the small volume of oxygen lost to the outside world. She watched him through the dome wall, fogged by years of scratches and scuffmarks, as he jumped in and started up the vehicle with a throaty roar. The cat's tracks kicked up dirt and dust as it turned and began to roll up the slope of the rocky outcrop towards the distant silhouette of Ellie perched like a spike of wind-eroded rock.

Shona arrived at her mother's elbow and watched the cat recede. 'Mum, are they boyfriend and girlfriend?'

'I hope not dear, otherwise I think Ellie's in for a lot of heartache.'

*

The peace and quiet of the overlook was shattered by the noise of the cat as it laboured up towards the rocky peak. Ellie watched Sean steer it up towards her. Presently he brought the vehicle to a stop a few yards away, turned off the rotor engine and climbed out, this time wearing his mask.

'Hiya Ellie…whaddya do out here? It seems like you spend most of your spare time up on this rock.'

77

'I think. It's my contemplation rock.'

He took in the view, slowly turning around a full three hundred and sixty degrees. 'What a view. I didn't realize how cool it was.'

'Now you can see why I spend so much time up here.'

He focused on a shimmering form on the horizon. 'What's that?'

'New Haven. It's the very top of the enviro-dome.'

'Wow, you can see it from here? That's hundreds of miles away.'

'Yup, a long, long way.'

He sat down beside her. The rock she was sat on was worn to a smooth shiny surface by the persistent sand erosion and, no doubt by Ellie, he guessed.

'Further to our discussion last time. I was thinking we should maybe wait until *after* your birthday before leaving.'

'You're not getting cold feet?'

'No, of course not. We're still going but delaying until after your birthday makes sense.'

She looked at him suspiciously. 'Why?'

'It's only delaying things by one more week, and being twenty means you won't need an adult sponsor for a lot of things. You'll be legally an adult yourself.' He shrugged. 'It'll just make things a lot easier with city red tape if you're no longer a minor.'

'What's red tape?'

Sean shook his head and smiled patronizingly at her. 'You are so-o-o-o-o lucky to have me around to explain things. In New Haven you can't even piss without having your ident card ready to show, swipe or have scanned. That's 'red tape'. I already have one since I've been there before. You'll have to get one when you arrive, that means presenting your birth document, listing details of next of kin, which will lead to all sorts of awkward questions if you're still only nineteen.'

'I see.'

They sat in silence for a while listening to the subdued melancholic wailing of wind across the featureless rust landscape.

'So, how are we getting there?' asked Ellie.

'Hmmm, it's a bit of a haul I'm afraid. We'll be taking a shuttle…'

'I was assuming you'd drive us there in this,' Ellie gestured towards the cat.

'No. She's only got a sixty-mile range between charges. We'll need to head towards a shuttle stopover. The nearest one is actually fifty miles northwest...'

'That's taking us in the wrong direction!'

'I know, I know, but that's the way it is. There are none any closer to New Haven. So anyway, it's a fifty mile drive and my Dad will be driving us.'

She looked alarmed. 'He doesn't know I'm going does he?'

'Of course not. Which means I'm going to have to smuggle you into the luggage locker. A bit of an uncomfortable ride, I'm afraid, but it is sealed so you won't have to wear a mask. The day we leave I'll drive over here and pick you up; I'll tell Dad I've come over to say 'bye to you guys. Then we head back to home, by the time we get back, you'll be hidden in the locker and Dad should be ready to take us to the shuttle-stop.'

'When exactly?'

'We'll go a week tomorrow.'

It was going to be the day after her birthday. All of a sudden, she now had a specific day she was leaving. Departure day. D-day. She leant forward on her elbows and puffed out some air. Her plastic O2 mask fogged.

'You okay?' asked Sean.

'Just excited, a bit nervous maybe. I just can't believe we're going to do this.'

He placed a hand on her shoulder and squeezed. She shivered. Partly a small thrill from his touch, but mostly from the exhilaration she felt discussing the journey ahead of her.

'We should arrange a time now, Ellie, since I probably won't get a chance to see you again before then.'

'Yay. No more math.'

'Six o'clock okay? First light?'

'I'll be ready. Where?'

He looked around the almost featureless landscape.

'Right up here looks the best bet, I reckon. It's far enough away from your home that the cat's engine won't wake everyone up.'

'Six o'clock right here, a week tomorrow?'

He nodded.

'And Ellie, make sure you bring your birth document and study certificates. You'll especially need the certificates if you want to find yourself a job.'

'Okay.'

Ellie hadn't given a great deal of thought to the type of job she would like. She was not at all sure what sort of jobs existed in New Haven. 'What do people do in the city?'

'You mean what work is there?'

She nodded.

'Well, it depends on which area you want to live in I guess. Central One area is mainly commerce, which is data work as far as you're concerned. How's your psyc-typing?'

Ellie wrinkled her nose. 'Not too good, my mind wanders.'

'Fair enough. Near the space port, which is the east side, you'll find jobs are more manual, cargo handling. But then they have gene-imps doing a lot of that kind of work.'

'Those little monkey-like things?'

'Yeah. They're very strong. They call them *jimps*. I guess that's short for 'gene-imp'. The west end of town is more your service sector...the rough side of the tracks.'

'Tracks?'

'Old Earth saying. Never mind,' he said dismissing the antiquated turn of phrase.

'You just probably want to steer clear of that.'

Ellie cocked an eyebrow. 'Service sector?'

'Bars, nightclubs, flesh markets. Trust me, not the sort of place you want to hang around. That's where you'll find the majority of off-worlders.'

'And aliens?'

'Yup, a few.'

'I've never seen an alien. Well, sure I've seen them on the toob, but never in person, face to face. Have you?'

'A couple of times when my Dad took me to the west end. Kinda freaky. I mean, I guess you must get used to them if you live around them all the time, but some of them are just too damn weird. There's this one kind, they call them 'boojams'. They've got these long trunk-like noses that sniff pheromones. Basically that's how they communicate amongst their own, by sniffing each other's sweat.'

Ellie chuckled. Getting to meet off-worlders was going to be a wonderful experience. Humans from other planets with vastly different cultures, accents and mannerisms would be fascinating, but then again, seeing *aliens* and maybe even talking with them was going to be something she would relish forever.

'I can't wait to meet some,' she said.

'Well, one step at a time, Ellie. You're gonna find city folk strange enough let alone other species.'

She was looking at something on the horizon. Sean followed her gaze. To the west the normally sharply defined horizon seemed slightly softened, almost like a section of the horizon had gone subtly out of focus.

'Dust storm,' she said. 'We better head inside.'

'About time anyway. If we stayed up here much longer, tongues would have started wagging.'

Ellie looked at him. 'I presume you mean Shona?'

He nodded. They got up off the rock and headed towards the buggy. The wind was beginning to pick up. Ellie glanced towards the approaching storm. The sky was darkening.

CHAPTER 9

The alarm clock chimed with a soft, persistent tone and Ellie was awake almost instantly. She raised an arm. The clock's motion sensor detected the movement and the holographic time display appeared in the middle of her habi-cube.

Ten past five in the morning. Sean was due in fifty minutes.

She climbed out of bed and silently dressed by the faint orange glow of the clock's display. She pulled a shoulder bag out from under her bed and double-checked the contents; birth document and educational certificates, her money, voice-diary and several changes of clothes. Anything else would be merely dead weight, emotional clutter. Sean had told her to pack very little and travel light. The ticket price for the shuttle to New Haven would be extremely expensive however the surcharge on baggage weight would be astronomical.

There was little that Ellie felt she would want to bring anyway.

She zipped up the bag and slung it over her shoulder and was almost out of her cabin before she remembered her promise to Sean. From her desk drawer she pulled a mem-card out of her writing tablet and left it on her pillow where it would not easily be missed. She had written a brief note to Mum and Dad letting them know where she was going, apologizing for leaving this way and promising to write or call as soon as she was settled.

She had surprised herself with a few guilty tears whilst writing her letter...guilt for running out on them like this, without a hug or a kiss or a goodbye. She assured them she was going to be in good hands, Sean was with her, and helping her settle into the city. She cast one final glance around her room.

Not much to show for the twenty years of her life. Jonny, her stuffed tartan sausage dog, sat morosely on the end of her bed, one large cloth ear drooped miserably over his sewn-on button eyes. She picked him up and pushed him carefully into her bag. Jonny, threadbare and faded, had dutifully provided her comfort through her childhood years, soaking up tears and snot, patiently tolerating her baby gums and playing the silent participant in many a game of tug of war. She decided after so many years of sterling service, it was only fair he got to come along for the ride too.

Ellie tiptoed across the courtyard towards her dome, Betsy. As she pushed through the curtain of dangling plastic flaps she felt the warm humidity wrap itself around her. She checked the time again; it was fifteen minutes past the hour. She headed towards the exit hatch where her mask and O2 cylinder hung. She had refilled the cylinder last night so that it would give her a full hour and a half of oxygen. As she walked alongside a row of tubweeds one of them casually lashed out with its pod, catching her.

'Ow! You little-,'

She felt her cheek. A small bump was beginning to rise. She decided there was enough time to indulge in one final, long overdue bit of payback.

'Okay you pathetic little weed, if that's how you want to thank me for all the tender loving care I've given you and your brothers, fine. This is how I'm going to thank you,' she hissed under her breath, reached down to the base of the plant and began pulling it up out of the soil.

'This is for all the stings, the hassle and generally being a nasty, shitty little plant.'

The tubweed began to writhe and twist in her hands, the pod swinging furiously, searching for a target. She heard the roots begin to snap beneath the soil. With one final tug she wrenched the plant out of the soil bed and threw it down on to the rubber matt floor of the dome. It continued to writhe pathetically for a few moments. The plant's central stalk began to bend and it slowly curled up into what appeared to be a disturbingly good imitation of a human fetal position.

She felt a twinge of guilt at that.

As she continued down the row of plants towards the hatch, the other tubweeds swayed backwards slightly, keeping a respectful distance from her. It dawned on her that maybe Ted and Shona had at some point made an early sacrificial example of one of their plants and that was why their crops always seemed to behave so well for them.

Typical. She sighed. *So NOW they want to be good little plants.*

Well it was too late; a week of Ted's heavy-handed care and they would all be pining for the good old days of Ellie's tender regime.

She reached the hatchway, lifted her mask and cylinder off the hook and put it on. She turned around to take one last look at her dome. She hoped that Dad's resolve to change things over would persist. At a time when the population was increasing dramatically, this world's ability to feed itself was met only through the costly importation of synthetic protein from other worlds. Now was the time to be a farmer growing a food crop, not oxygen-farming. Soon, maybe as little as twenty to thirty years from now, the air on Harpers Reach would be enough that the enviro-domes planet-wide would be thrown off or torn down.

She opened the hatch and quickly slipped out, closing it promptly behind her. As the hatch clicked and sealed with a hiss Ellie felt an overpowering surge of excitement.

'Despite a hesitant start, Ms Ellie Quin is off the starting block and under way,' she muttered quietly with a smile, vaguely remembering a children's story about a hare and a tortoise.

She started to make her way up the rocky slope to the overlook. The purple night sky was beginning to lighten and the horizon to the north glowed with the distinctive pink of dawn approaching. Daylight was still an hour and a half away. She checked the time again. There were still thirty minutes until Sean was due. She was glad. That would give her a quiet half-hour to say goodbye to her home and family and this all-too small world of hers…and time to look towards the south and contemplate the new, much larger world ahead.

*

'Come on Sean, where the freg are you?!'

Ellie checked the time again. It was nearly seven. The horizon was growing brighter and the new day was fast approaching. She strained her eyes to look for the telltale dust trail of his dirt-cat. She could see none. The air in her cylinder was not going to last much longer. She would have to head back down to the farm and get another one pretty soon. Ellie bit her lip in frustration. It was typical of her luck. He had arrived promptly for every study lesson she had had with him over the last four years, today he should bloody well choose to be late.

No choice. She decided to head back for some more oxygen right now whilst her family were still asleep rather than delay any longer. She scanned the horizon one last time.

Nothing.

'Dammit.'

She let herself into the domestic dome as quietly as she could. She couldn't hear any noises coming from Ted's cabin, and he was always the first one up. She crept stealthily across the courtyard towards Shona's dome. Beside her exit hatch there would be another oxygen cylinder. It would undoubtedly be full of oxygen since Shona rarely bothered with going outside. But it would also be horribly stale since she probably hadn't checked it in months.

Ellie passed by the kitchen habi-cube and heard the soft digital chime of the v-phone. Someone had left a message.

Sean.

She entered the kitchen, dark except for one small safety strip-light that buzzed irritatingly. She approached the phone with a sinking heart. The display showed there was only one message, with Sean's family home number beside it. Ellie hit the 'play' button.

There was Sean's voice only, no holo image.

'I'm really sorry...really sorry Ellie. There's no easy way of saying this so I guess I'll just come out with it. We've just been contacted. The Freezer's arrived early and they're calling in all the Harper's Reach recruits. I've got to go right now. It only stays in port for twenty-four hours...I can't afford to miss it. Ellie, I made you a promise and now I have to break it, which makes me feel like a complete dreg-head. So, I'm going to make you a brand new one, okay? And this is it...I will come back to you at the end of the tour of duty in eight years and I promise you that I will take you anywhere you want to go: New Haven, off-world, anywhere. Okay? We'll travel, we'll see as much of this universe as you want. And we'll be together. Christ...I'll marry you. Okay? I've got to go now. Dad's warming up the buggy. I'll write when I can.'

There was a pause. Ellie could hear his panting breath, he'd obviously been running around making frantic preparations. In the background she could hear the rotor engine revving and the sound of Sean's mother sobbing.

'Ellie, do this one thing for me please. Don't go to New Haven alone, okay?'

The line stayed open a few seconds more. She heard his father gunning the throttle impatiently.

'I'll see you around.'

And the message ended.

Ellie stared at the blinking message indicator. It was silent in the kitchen, save for the intermittent buzzing of the safety light. The kitchen smelled of curry. Mum had cooked Balusa curry cakes for her birthday party yesterday. What a pitifully sad party that had been; Mum, Dad, Ted, Shona and two of Shona's friends from a farm nearby and, of course, Ellie herself who, it seemed, had no friends of her own to invite. She would have invited Sean, but given their plans for this morning...

The light continued to blink.

Her twentieth birthday party was marked by a bowl of punch, some curry cakes and an awkward rendition of 'happy birthday', after which Shona and her gang retired to her habi-cube and Ted to a corner of the courtyard to watch a cartoon. Mum and Dad dutifully hung around sipping punch and making small talk, trying their best to look like a party in full swing.

Traditionally, her next big birthday party would be twenty-one. Ellie grimly imagined how pathetic that would be too and wondered whether by then she might have managed to get to know somebody well enough to invite.

Wow…a guest of my own.

The light continued to blink like a warning beacon.

If you don't get out now girl, you never will.

She hit the delete button on the phone. The message was gone. Sean was never going to keep that promise anyway.

*

Ellie stood beside the caterpillar. It had blown a primer six weeks ago. Dad had tried to repair it but, basically, it needed to be replaced. He had tried to find a spare primer at the trade fair but to no avail. Sand had built up over the canvas sheeting that covered it. She lifted one corner of the cover and shook enough of it free to throw it back, exposing the driver's side hatch.

She looked again at the time. Twenty minutes had passed since she'd last checked. The deep purple of the night sky was lightening quickly, heralding the arrival of the sun over the horizon. Ted must surely be stirring by now, she thought.

Ellie opened the hatch and climbed inside. She was looking for two things. She found the first one in the emergency box. It was an oxy-filter. It had a battery pack that lasted about twenty hours and recycled oxygen as long as the power lasted. The other thing she was looking for was the navset; a small box that gave global positioning co-ordinates and also functioned as an emergency beacon. She found this in the passenger-seat storage compartment. She flicked it on. It worked, but the battery indicator was requesting a charge. It would probably be okay for the short period of time she would need it to be on she thought. She slid the navset into her bag and slung the oxy-filter over her shoulder. Ellie planned to use Shona's O2 cylinder until it was empty before switching to the filter.

She climbed back out of the caterpillar, pulled the canvas cover back down and started up towards the overlook.

At the top she looked briefly back down at the farm. 'I'll see you around.'

Ellie faced south and for the first time considered the dusty rocky world ahead. It sloped down from the overlook and evened out. In front of her lay an almost infinite plain of dust and clay, punctuated by the occasional cluster of weatherworn rocks, like islands in an ocean of rust-red, that cast long streaky shadows as the sun breached the horizon.

'My god, this is so-o-o-o-o stupid.'

She took her first step down the far-side slope.

CHAPTER 10

Aaron Goodman travelled alone.

It had taken him fifteen years of working for Oxxon as a driver to save up the money to buy his lovely, beautiful baby, *Lisa*. Of course, to anyone else *Lisa* appeared to be a shabby-looking, thirty-year old transport tug. To Aaron, it was a home as well as head office for *Goodman Haulage Inc*. It represented fifteen years of hard work and frugal living and was a monument to the single-mindedness and sheer determination of Aaron Goodman to work wholly for himself, and entirely by himself.

To be fair, *Lisa* did look a little threadbare and shabby, but she was a firmly built working ship with a well-maintained propulsion system. Quietly, he liked the fact that her hull was scoured clean of paint through years of exposure to wind-borne sand, that her once smooth and eye-pleasing contours were dented and spoiled through countless minor bumps and prangs with other working ships or docking clamps. The dull brown, pitted hull told any onlooker that she was a working vessel, that she had probably seen considerably more of this world than most other vessels her age - which, quite frankly, was a sad comment on the pioneering spirit of most of the moronic slobs that lived on Harpers Reach.

Colonists were not the same these days, he noted ruefully. Once upon a time they were the kind of people who would happily endure the hardships of frontier life. They were the pack-horse, the mule, the beast of burden of the terra-forming process, only content with their lives when stoically enduring some form of physical discomfort or inconvenience. Once upon a time the Crazy People, the Mom-and-Pop teams of geologists, the frontier-professionals, *real Colonists*, would make it their mission to seek out the most extreme hardship Human Space could offer and then relish every moment of it. And it was crazies like those that turned a barren inhospitable lump of sulphurous rock into a world that comfortably supported human life.

Real colonists.

These days the unwashed masses, those brain-flatlined ditto-heads who presumptuously referred to themselves as 'colonists' were perfectly content to crowd themselves into the nearest domed city they could find on arrival. There, they were happy to live out their pointless, unadventurous lives eating junk food and watching the toob, certainly not daring to set a foot beyond the environmentally-sealed comfort and convenience of their newly discovered plastic dome-home. Not for them the hardy living within the cramped space of a caterpillar or shuttle, or the danger that comes with exploring the uncharted continents of a new world. No way. These pasty-faced, convenience-fed, brain-dead, ditto-heads were quite content to enjoy the homogenous pleasures of yet another enclosed over-crowded conurbation and leave the real work of building a new world to the likes of grubby looking veterans like Aaron Goodman.

He had spent a good chunk of his working life shipping supplies and spare parts into the Oxxon oxygen refineries in the north. The refineries required a permanent on-site team of engineers to monitor and maintain the enormous generators there. All-in-all, there were ninety-seven people, including the non-technical support staff, living up north in the austere living quarters built by the company over one hundred and fifty years ago. Although the living quarters, service buildings and the machinery that powered the oxygen refineries were built to last such periods of time, inevitably, now towards the latter end of their intended functional lifespan the rate of component failure for these structures was quite high. The constant maintenance and repair tasks carried out by the engineering team over time were being gradually down-graded to temporary 'fix-its'.

It was a running joke amongst the maintenance engineers that when the refineries were finally mothballed, they would probably find the whole thing was held together with tape and string.

Everything those folks needed for a tolerably comfortable life needed to be shipped in. Aaron had once upon a time been employed as a delivery driver for Oxxon. Now he worked freelance for them, and the shuttle that was once theirs, he had bought for a song - all part of the inevitable downsizing as the refinery approached the end of its useful life. Where once there was a large team of drivers ferrying supplies up north, now it was just Aaron and his weather-beaten shuttle.

Lisa was a hundred and fifty foot long, low-altitude, transport shuttle. Her top speed was five hundred and twenty miles per hour, but her most economic speed was just over two hundred miles per hour. Aaron flew her low, very low. He did that to catch the densest strata of atmosphere, riding the top of it like a cushion, making the most of the free buoyancy. It gave him the most uplift for the least fuel burn. Generally speaking, when he needed to sleep he let the auto-pilot fly her at an altitude of two or three hundred feet, to be safe. If he was at the helm he would skim her sometimes as low as fifty feet off the ground.

A trip up to the Oxxon refineries usually took five days going up and four days coming back down to New Haven. Every now and then Aaron would delay the return trip a day or so. He loved the arctic terrain, the unspoiled sheets of ice and snow up north. It was, he reckoned, the only beautiful wilderness on the entire planet and one day it would all be gone as the atmosphere thickened, the world retained more of its heat and it melted away. It was a pretty depressing prospect to him that the only truly beautiful place on this ugly mud ball planet would be sacrificed to produce a breathable atmosphere so that hordes of miserable, so-called 'colonists' could spill out of New Haven and fill it up with their unimaginative and ugly homes.

And when that finally happened Aaron Goodman would go and take his haulage business to some new frontier world and enjoy another beautiful and remote wilderness waiting to be terraformed to death.

Sometimes he would take his shuttle a few hours further north of the refineries until he could see them no more and then set her down on the virgin snow. Often he camped out over night in the open, nothing but a heated therma-bag to sleep in and a flask of coffee for company. There was no need for an O2 mask or a small, sealed one man dome-tent, up here. The atmosphere was oxygen-rich. He would study the crisp night sky, and pretend he was some ancient Old Earth explorer marking time on a drifting iceberg in the frozen seas of Earth's South Pole.

*

Okay, yes…I'm beginning to panic.

The plan had been to walk for a couple of hours, then flag the first low altitude craft she saw with her navset. Ellie figured she could hash together some vague story about crashing a dune buggy and seeking help on foot. The crew that picked her up might be conscientious enough to try and locate it with her pointing the way, but of course they would never find the wreckage and then of course they would be obliged to drop her off at their destination.

Hopefully New Haven.

She had been walking in a southerly direction for nearly eighteen hours now and had not seen a single craft. She was beginning to wonder whether she had drifted off course and was heading away from New Haven and thus away from the converging routes used by the various transport craft that crisscrossed the planet. Add to that she'd consumed most of the water she had brought with her and the recycler was only going to give her another two to three hours of breathable air.

To be honest, it was looking a little bit like she was going to die.

Great.

Ellie was going to die out here in the middle of nowhere and no-one was ever going to find her body. The message she had left behind at home unambiguously announced that she had run away to New Haven and would get in touch again when she was settled. Mum and Dad would be worried, and they might even be able to bribe the over-worked and undermanned and generally disinterested police force in New Haven to put out a missing person bulletin for her. But of course they would be looking in the city instead of out here in the middle of nowhere where her bones would slowly bleach in the sun and eventually be covered by sand.

Maybe some archaeologist in the distant future might discover her, but Mum and Dad sure as hell would not.

She slumped to her knees and started to whimper.

'Stupid girl. You and your stupid dream. You've killed yourself, that's what you've done.'

She pulled Jonny out of the bag and held him to her face. She closed her eyes and rocked gently. It was all over, before it had even fregging well got started. Tears of anger and frustration streamed down her face and she lay down on the ground hugging the stuffed dog.

'A loser's death, you're a stupid loser,' she muttered to herself.

Half an hour passed and Ellie allowed herself to drift off to sleep. She figured it might be less distressing if her recycler were to run out of power whilst she was asleep. To die that way had to be better than struggling consciously with every breath and experiencing the muscular spasms of oxygen starvation.

There was a distant rumble.

Her face jerked upwards. Her eyes opened and darted left and right desperately seeking the source of the noise. She saw it, the subtle glimmer of a thrust jet; a space-faring vessel entering orbit. It was a long way out, maybe too far to pick up the signal. But it was the only thing she had seen all day. Ellie decided to switch on the navset beacon for a few seconds.

It started to blink silently.

For a full two minutes she watched the space vessel as it slowly traced a line across the sky. She knew enough to know that if it could have received the signal the onboard navigational system would have already noted it and logged the co-ordinates. She turned off the navset to conserve its batteries. If the signal had been detected then there was a fair chance the ship might detour and investigate or dispatch a smaller surface ship to go and take a look.

Never underestimate the pulling power of salvage rights. That was something Dad had once said whilst he'd been checking the navset's power supply.

*

A light blinked on his navigation dash. Aaron looked down at it, it was an emergency beacon. The signal only lasted a minute or so, but it was enough time for him to register the point of origin. He adjusted course slightly, it was only fifteen miles north-east - the distances he was used to travelling, that wasn't exactly out of his way. And anyway, legislation on New Haven still permitted the universally accepted forty percent salvage law. Aaron rubbed his rough hands together and smiled.

'Bonus time.'

He swung the shuttle round to a north-easterly course. The terrain ahead was as flat as a table top, sun baked clay with scattered rocks as far as the eye could see. Aaron was cruising at fifty feet. He decided to bring her up to get a better view of the area ahead. He could be looking for anything, something as small as a crashed or broken down personal transport to a shuttle the same size as his. He pulled back on the yoke and the rust-colored ground beneath quickly fell away. The altitude display showed one hundred and eighty feet. That was enough. He leveled off and started to scan for an early visual; a distant column of smoke; an impact scorch trail. Something. He checked the logged co-ordinates of the beacon, it was just over ten miles away.

*

Ellie watched in disbelief as the orbital freighter continued across to the southern horizon's darkening sky and flickered momentarily as it finally exited the planet's upper atmosphere.

'What about me?' she muttered indignantly.

A wind was beginning to pick up and she shuddered. The nights could get very cold out in the open. Very cold. Once again she reminded herself what a sad specimen she was for not preparing properly and bringing something more substantial than the clothes she had thrown on this morning.

Then a small light on the recycler's battery pack winked on.

'Oh..great.'

It was the low charge warning. She wondered how much stored power was left. Another half hour, or another minute? She decided to try her luck with the air. The wind was cold, it could be an oxygen pocket. She tentatively pulled the mask away from her face and took several deep breaths. A minute passed before she began to feel dizzy and nauseous and hurriedly pulled the mask back on. She frantically scanned the sky and the horizon.

Nothing.

She pulled out the navset again. This time she was not quite so worried about its battery life, the way things were going it would probably outlive her. She turned it on and set it down on the ground beside her. She lay down in the dust and turned her head to face the little black box. Its one green blinking light was a strange comfort in the gathering darkness.

The sun was breaching the horizon, swiftly on its way down and out of sight. Ellie watched as the amber circle undulated and rippled like a slick of oil on water as it descended from view. Over the space of five minutes the peach after-glow it left faded and the golden ribbon emerged like the king of the night sky, and one by one, like loyal subjects, the stars followed it.

Ellie thought of Sean. He'd probably be in New Haven right now, boarding a shuttle to take him to the huge mother-ship in orbit. What a fantastic experience that was going to be for him. To see through a viewing bay, your whole world and everything you have ever known and to watch it gradually recede and become simply a glowing disc, eventually a mere pin-prick.

At least one of them had escaped the gravitational pull of Harpers Reach. 'Lucky you, Sean...you did it.' There was surprisingly no bitterness in that. She was genuinely pleased for him.

The light on the recycler changed color. It had been green and now it had changed to red. She heard the thin reedy whine she had grown used to inside the recycler drop in tone and then cease. The red light then dimmed and finally went out.

This is it then.

The air in the mask and the machine's 'lungs' would last her another minute or so then quickly degrade. She found herself thinking…

Actually, I'm not scared.

Ellie smiled. In the last minutes of her life she decided she'd discovered a profound truth, a little gem of wisdom that she would have liked to pass on to the countless millions of other pointless losers like her in the universe.

It really isn't that bad…dying.

*

Aaron Goodman switched on the floods and descended to thirty feet as he approached. The beacon had come on again. By now he reckoned he should soon be able to pick out the dark form of any vehicle against the lighter ground. But he could see nothing yet.

The range marker began counting down the distance in hundreds of feet.

…eighteen hundred feet…

…sixteen hundred feet…

…fourteen hundred feet...

He could see nothing. He cut the speed and engaged vertical thrust to prevent the shuttle stalling and dropping. The large vehicle now pushed forward at a crawl, its pug-faced cockpit dipping downwards. The shuttle rocked and wobbled uncertainly under momentum solely from the VTOL thrusters.

…Six hundred feet…

…five hundred feet…

…four hundred feet...

The floodlights panned across the ground, picking out nothing but the occasional sharp spur of weather-worn rock. He was virtually on top of the damned beacon but he couldn't see anything at all; no sign of a craft, crash damage, debris. Nothing.

'So how the hell does a beacon get out here on its own?' Aaron mumbled with growing irritation.

As the range marker counted down the last one hundred feet, his floodlights finally picked out what looked like a small body lying inert on the dusty ground.

He set the shuttle down.

CHAPTER 11

It happened from time to time, bad luck.

Life, no matter who you are or how important you are, deals out the crap pretty evenly.

Researcher Rowan Brown was pleased at the way that truism sounded. It had that kind of lived in feel, like an old saying, almost poetic. He made a mental note to try and slot it into the next conversation he was undoubtedly likely to have about his boss, the late Master Researcher, Dr Edward Mason.

Dr Mason died two days ago. Although the news was incomplete and had not officially been confirmed through normal channels, the story seemed to be that the transport ship carrying him down to Pacifica for a couple of weeks of sun and sea had lost its entry shield and disintegrated in the upper atmosphere. There had been twenty other workers from the Lab aboard and, of course, the flight crew. None of them had survived either, but the only name of significance and likely to be newsworthy when the story broke was that of Dr Mason.

Search and rescue teams had scanned the sea below the grid co-ordinate at which the craft had vanished. But being so high up, virtually in orbit, the debris spray radius was enormous. They had recovered the telemetry box which would have had a transmitter inside it, but found nothing else floating in the vicinity other than a twisted sheet of partially melted beige plastic that had been identified as a seat-mounted fold down table.

There had certainly been no bodies so far and there probably never would be. Pacifica was all water. Any sections of the transport ship that had survived the atmosphere were now at the bottom of a very deep ocean.

For now, and maybe a day or two more, the story was being kept quiet. It was looking like a simple case of component failure and not attracting any speculation from the search team that something amiss might have happened. But until that was properly confirmed, those who knew of the incident, like Rowan Brown and his colleagues, were under orders to keep their mouths shut.

Rowan had been working for Dr Mason for several years, enough time to get to know the old man quite well.

A brilliant man. But quite untidy.

Rowan Brown inserted his thumb into the DNA-scanner and felt the lightest touch of a sensor from inside the small panel mounted beside the door. A brief moment passed before the unit hummed an approval-tone and the door to Mason's personal research labs slid silently open.

Mason's death was going to make big news. No matter how innocuous the findings of the incident, the temptation for the media to go looking for a conspiracy theory once they found out about his death would be almost unbearable. Rowan figured, in the end, after months, maybe years of investigation and analysis of any crash debris they were lucky to find, the death of someone as important as Mason would probably all boil down to the failure of a ten credit component.

Life really does deal the crap out pretty evenly.

He passed by the late doctor's sealed workbench. He noticed some DNA sample slides were still inside and not locked away;

presumably work of Mason's that he'd left half-done. He could be like that. Untidy.

Rowan sighed tiredly. Tying up the loose ends and squaring everything away for Mason's successor – Rowan was hoping it was going to be him - was going to be a major pain in the ass. Dr Mason had been in this post for nearly thirty years. He'd left a lot of clutter, both intellectual and physical, to tidy up.

He stopped for another thumb-scan and a moment later the door to the doctor's inner-sanctum slid open.

Mason's study.

The old man had a taste for pre-colonial wars' hand-crafted furniture. Amidst the cool clinical blue walls and floors of the Department's orbiting laboratories, this room, full of faux rich mahogany wood, seemed utterly out of place. Rowan had always felt he was stepping into a holo-film set from the early twentieth century when he entered this room. The wood surfaces, of course, were all actually molded plasti-carbonite veneers. Even someone like Mason would find it difficult to justify the cost of shipping genuine wooden furniture across the galaxy.

A single wide portrait window behind his desk over-looked the brilliantly lit ocean world, Pacifica. The rich cerulean blue was lightly marbled with just a few threads of cloud. Beams of reflected sunlight poured through the broad window into the small dark room, bathing it in a rich, aquatic ambience.

On the desk was an ancient, twentieth century ink blotter and writing set. Dr Mason had always preferred reading reports on paper rather than on a holo-screen. It afforded him the pleasure of being able to make his notes in the traditional way. There was no doubting the satisfaction the man had derived from using his favorite antique fountain pen. Rowan noticed that the pen was gone.

Vaporized along with him, no doubt.

The desk was covered with paper. Half-read reports with query marks, words crossed out or underlined and tidy copperplate writing filling the margins. Rowan gathered together the papers on the desk, opened a desk drawer, hastily dropped the papers in and locked it. He would have to go through all those papers at some point in the near future and organize them for his next boss. But for now, Rowan felt it would be careless and vaguely disrespectful to leave them out.

'First things first,' he announced to himself.

He passed his hand over a lens embedded in the desk top and a holo-screen appeared in the air before him. Mason's access to the data server would need to be turned off from this terminal and any open or checked-out files closed and his user id number removed from the system for security reasons.

He trawled through Mason's directories one by one, closing files that had been left open - there were quite a few.

In Rowan's opinion, the late Doctor had few faults. The man had been a legend in the field of genetics and had run the Department for three decades with an efficiency that had been unprecedented, but, he was very careless and messy in the way he used the database. A bad habit that he must have developed over so many years with no-one brave enough to chastise him for his reckless data security infringements.

After a few minutes of tidying away Mason's virtual workspace he came across a password-protected directory. It had a name

117

that looked every bit as mundane as all the others.

[STATS-TEMP]

'That's very unlike you Doctor,' muttered Rowan. He was constantly being nagged by the Department's data security officer, to remind Mason to keep all his digital data locked away and password protected. But the old man shrugged that off. He never bothered with that. But this particular one, unlike most of the other folders, *was* closed and locked.

He frowned as he felt himself tugged unpleasantly between professional discretion and insatiable curiosity. It was locked, which meant it was private, even from the eyes of his immediate assistant Rowan Brown.

Private, as in, correspondence with a loved one?...poetry even?...personal essays?...pictures?...fantasies?

Mason had, after all, been just a man, flesh and blood. He had no wife, nor immediate family. In fact, he had been known to be a very solitary man. His work had been everything. If there had been a part of his life he had wished to remain secret, to

118

keep from the public domain, perhaps it was in there?

Rowan felt a guilty stab of curiosity.

'No, come on…the man has the right to privacy.'

He moved his hand across the shimmering holographic workspace towards the 'PURGE' button. Whatever the old man's secrets were, they would die with him. As his finger hovered over the holographic icon his curiosity took a hold of him once more.

Come on, how hard would it be to unlock it. Look inside. Just a glimpse? Hmm?

'Not very hard at all,' he answered himself. Mason was a compulsive note-taker, a man who undoubtedly would leave some sort of password prompt, a reminder, within convenient view of his desk; a soft target for a data-cracker.

He looked around. The walls were lined with books, another of Mason's antediluvian diversions. Many of them were replicas of famous ancient books from before the wars, before even the great Era of Expansion, back when humans were a one-world race. He cocked his head to read the gold-embossed words along the mock-leather spines.

119

Treasure Island, Peter Pan, The Lion, The Witch and the Wardrobe, Alice in Wonderland, Pinocchio.

The titles sounded childish to him, like nursery rhymes. He continued to scan the room. On the wall was a map of the constellations that effectively made up Human Space, beside that was an oil painting of Old Earth.

Rowan entered the word 'EARTH' on the keypad.

The directory remained closed. Not his password.

He quickly tried 'TERRA', 'GAIA', and 'HOME', but none of them had any affect either. Guilt for attempting to plunder the dead man's secrets finally got the better of him.

'Oh forget it,' he said under his breath and reached once more for the purge icon.

And it was then that he saw it.

The word was written discreetly in the corner of the blotter on the desk. The ink had faded and was a faint watery blue against the pink blotting paper. More recent drops of dark blue ink, scribblings and doodles adorned the pink surface, but this one word stood out for its faintness; a word written a long time ago.

He can't have been that careless surely?

Rowan entered the word 'Cassandra' and the folder opened and the data inside arranged itself across the holo-screen. He stared long and hard at the texts; the soul of Dr Mason laid bare, his thoughts, his anxieties, a stream of consciousness, essays, notes.

'Oh my God.'

CHAPTER 12

Ellie could smell coffee, strong and bitter.

She tried to sit up, but immediately she felt the ache of exhausted muscles complaining. Instead she settled for opening her eyes and found herself trying to focus on the underside of a dirty looking canvas hammock strung only a few inches above her. It was full, and swayed with a stressed creak. She looked down the length of the bulging, oil-stained canvas and saw a hairy leg dangling over the side. It reminded her of a shank of meat. The foot swung lazily in mid air and, from where she was, she could smell the damned thing.

She could hear music playing and vaguely recognized the track. It was something her Mum and Dad listened to, folksy and embarrassing. Above her, she heard a baritone voice rumbling tunelessly along with the music.

Rather than immediately alert whoever lay above her that she was awake, Ellie decided to keep quiet for the moment and get a better handle on her surroundings. It looked like the interior of a vessel of some kind. She had seen enough on the toob to guess that, and in any case she had already detected the subtle vibration and the deep throbbing rumble. She was in transit to somewhere.

Ellie had seen interiors like this in many a toob drama, from adventurous, edge-of-the-Universe scout ships to planet-hopping trade skiffs, usually piloted by some heroic flint-faced, chisel-jawed hunk. She cast her eyes up at the pendulous swinging bulge of the straining hammock. She couldn't imagine the leg dangling over the side belonged to someone like that.

In one of those stupid toob dramas she remembered a character saying something like '...pilot spends enough time out there, he ends up looking like his ship.'

She looked at the grubby interior around her; the improvised washing line suspended across the cabin and at the pasty colored shank of meat that was swaying casually in time with the music and guessed there might be some truth in that.

The hammock creaked alarmingly as the body above lurched without warning. A second leg appeared over the side and with a thud that rang through the metal floor of the cabin the hammock's occupant dropped into view.

He was tall. *Very* tall. And thickset. Perhaps that was muscle, perhaps he was overweight, she couldn't tell beneath the oil stained olive overalls he was wearing.

A coil of long light-colored curly hair hung over his face and he pulled it and the rest of his frizzy hair back into a bushy ponytail and pulled on a faded cap to keep the few stray locks out of his face. His cheeks sported several days' worth of blonde fuzz.

A buzzer sounded and he leant across a bank of lights and switches to hit a button. A flap opened revealing a steaming decanter of stewed coffee and he turned towards Ellie. She snapped her eyes shut.

'You want some?' he grunted.

She did her best to maintain the appearance of being in a deep sleep, fighting with her eyelids to stop them fluttering and giving her away.

'It's okay, you know? Reheated...sure, but it's still coffee. Well,' he added in a baritone voice that sounded almost as deep as the vehicle's engine. '*Almost* coffee.'

Ellie maintained her silence and her stillness, breathing deeply.

'Fair enough,' he said gruffly, pouring out a mug and turning to make his way forward from the narrow confines of the bunk area towards the even tighter space of the vessel's cockpit.

'Do you have any milk?' Ellie asked hopefully.

The pilot stopped and looked back at her. 'Oh? It's alive, *and* it talks. Incredible.'

He carried on manoeuvring through an obstacle course of boxed supplies, holding his mug high like a trophy, past a makeshift repair bench before easing himself carefully into the pilot's seat. Ellie was impressed at the grace and agility of his performance - not a single drop spilled.

'Sure, I got milk,' he shouted back at her over his shoulder. 'It's proto-milk, though.'

Ellie wrinkled her nose. *Proto, great.*

Her stomach grumbled. She was hungry, very hungry. 'You don't have any cereal do you?'

Aaron nodded. 'Yeah, I've got a packet of those Puffs with them marshmallow bits in, if you want some of that.'

'Solar Nuggatz?'

'Yeah that's the stuff.'

Ellie smiled. They were Ted's favorite. She swung her legs off the bunk and sat up. Her head was throbbing and her arms and legs ached intensely - a testament of how close she had come to atmospheric poisoning and asphyxiation. With a great deal of effort she stood up and shuffled towards what appeared to be 'the galley'. She found a hatch, opened it and pulled out a box of cereal. The free toy inside was Trac Plasma, a simple unarticulated mould of one of the characters from Ted's favorite show. Trac, or 'the green one' as she referred to him, seemed to be the one found in most boxes of Solar Nuggatz; the other three Plasma Rangers seemed to be a rarity.

'You got a *Trac*,' she announced, not sure if he'd know what she was talking about.

'Yup, seems like that little green bastard's in every damn packet,' he replied over his shoulder.

Aaron watched her as she searched for a bowl. Then turned back and sipped his coffee whilst he checked the autopilot log for anything of interest. Whilst he'd been asleep there had been no significant events. The shuttle had covered just over two thousand miles at a cruise speed of three hundred miles per hour and an altitude of three hundred feet. One other shuttle had been detected briefly twelve hundred miles away and had tried making radio contact five times with the call sign 'Ivory'.

Someone after a bit of company.

All in all it had been another typical night. Typical that is, except for finding this girl in the middle of nowhere and about two or three breaths away from permanent brain damage; and he wasn't entirely sure yet whether or not the girl had taken a hit on that front. Aaron had quite a few questions lined up for her just as soon as she'd had something to eat and drink.

A moment later she squeezed past the repair bench and attempted to sit down in the co-pilot's chair.

'Uh…just a moment,' he said. He reached across and swept a clutter of food wrappers and other rubbish that had built up there onto the floor.

Ellie sat down, conscious of the fact that the seat was worn through in several places, and in one spot an uncomfortable-looking spring was exposed. They sat in silence for a while accompanied only by the deep and strangely comforting rumble of the shuttle's engines.

'Thank you,' she said eventually. 'You know, for saving me….and for breakfast.'

Aaron said nothing, he continued studying the autopilot's log.

Ellie looked out of the cockpit windows. It was pitch black outside. She couldn't recall ever having seen a night so dark.

'It's so dark out there. I didn't realize it was night,' she said in an anxious bid to break-ice with the man.

He absent-mindedly reached up and hit a switch on a panel above his seat. She heard a subdued whine, and almost immediately a blinding strip of light appeared along the bottom of each window as the blast shields outside slid upwards. She covered her face from the unbearable glare with her hands as the strip of bright light slowly widened and the cockpit became bathed with the heat and brilliance of the early morning sun. The whining ended with a clunk and tentatively she unscrewed her eyes and lowered her arms.

'Uh, okay, I see.'

Three hundred feet below, the sun-baked clay desert rushed beneath them. She leant forward in her seat to get a better view.

'So how old are you? Fourteen? Fifteen?' asked Aaron.

'Twenty,' she answered briskly.

'Twenty?!' Aaron spurted coffee from his lips. 'Yeah right, and I'm six and a half. Let's try that again shall we?'

'I am!' she replied, her voice rising anxiously. 'I had a birthday yesterday.'

He cocked an eyebrow and the patronizing smile on his face widened as she maintained a hurt, indignant expression on her face. 'No! Really…I am. I've got citizenship papers to prove it.'

He studied her closely and eventually conceded she might just possibly be that old at a pinch. Out-city kids seemed to age slower than city brats. She was scrawny – that was the word. *Scrawny*. Straight up and down, short hair like a boy and the sun-darkened upper face of someone who spent a lot of time outside with an O2 mask.

'Okay, you can show me your papers later. But you can tell me now what the Hell you were doing out there on your own,' he shook his head in disbelief, 'and on foot for chrissakes!'

Ellie was about to start telling her carefully rehearsed story about the buggy breaking down and how she set out on foot to seek help, but despite having practiced the story over and over whilst she'd been out there walking, it all sounded a little bit silly and unconvincing now.

'I ran away from home.'

He nodded slowly. That made sense. 'Lemme' guess....farm kid right?'

Ellie nodded mutely.

'Heading for New Haven?'

She nodded once more, and smiled sheepishly. 'Are we nearly there yet?'

'Nope, not even close.'

'Uh?'

'That's because we're not heading towards New Haven,' he added. 'We're heading away.'

She turned sharply in her seat to face him. 'Not going to New Haven?! No, oh no, I was nearly there!'

Aaron laughed. 'You were nowhere near young lady. I found you two hundred and seventy miles out from Haven, and right now we're about four thousand miles from that crap-ola city.'

She slumped in her seat unhappily.

Aaron glanced at her, she was a pitiful sight. A child that had run away from home for whatever reason and fallen flat on her face at the very first hurdle. 'Okay listen, we'll be heading back that way in a few days time,' he added.

Ellie sat up and turned towards him, 'when?'

'Like I said, a few days. Maybe a week.'

'So where are you going now?'

Aaron grinned, a wide smile spread across a bristly face. 'We're heading somewhere about a billion times better than New Haven.'

Ellie waited for the man to elaborate, but he didn't. She tried to imagine where on the planet could possibly be a billion times better than the planet's one main city. Clearly he wasn't going to add any more to that. A surprise then. Another, more important question, occurred to her.

'What are you going to do with me?'

'Well now…that depends. If you're really as old as you say you are then I guess on the way back I can drop you off in New Haven, if that's what you want. If you're not twenty, then I'm obliged to either return you to your parents or hand you over to the authorities so they can send you back. But right now, we're heading north. I've got a scheduled shipment to make and I can't afford any detours or delays. Understand?'

Ellie nodded, 'okay.'

She started to eat her cereal and spilled milk from the first spoonful down her chin as the shuttle bumped over a pocket of dense air. She pretended to gaze out of the cockpit window at the drab landscape whipping by as she tucked into her breakfast. But out of the corner of her eye she studied him as he meticulously checked a screen full of data. She found herself relaxing a little. This tall man with his faded cap and mop of scruffy blonde hair, his seven-day stubble and oil stained clothes seemed to be a decent enough sort.

He finally snapped off the data screen and turned to Ellie holding out a large hand towards her. 'Since we're on talking terms now, I suppose I better know your name. I'm Aaron Goodman.'

'Ellie Quin,' she replied grabbing his large rough hand and shaking it gently. She giggled at the formal gesture.

'Well Ms Quin, tell me...do you like snow?'

'Snow?' She had to think about the word for a while before an image came to mind. 'Do you mean the white stuff you see on some worlds, like sugar?'

'That's right. You ever seen it for yourself?'

'Only on the toob Mr Goodman. It looks fantastic, sort of magical like fairy dust.' She grimaced slightly at the childish simile.

Aaron laughed. 'In that case you're going to love where we're going, and listen...lose the *Mr Goodman* crap....you can call me Captain. Or call me Aaron. Those are the options.'

CHAPTER 13

It never ceased to amaze him how quickly people can adapt to a new routine in their life. Routines, habits, patterns of behavior were a bit like music, he had decided once. They had a rhythm, a pace, even a melody of sorts, and how easy it was, it seemed, to go from humming one song to humming the next. On these regular delivery runs up to the refineries in the north, Aaron found that he always seemed to leave New Haven with a song or tune lodged in his head like an unwelcome guest. It would rattle around between his ears hour after hour, day after day, driving him mad with the repetition. But it only took a bar or two of some new catchy tune to drive it out for good, even if the damned thing had been holding his sanity hostage for several days. And life, he decided, was a little like that. It can be the same for years and years, the routine never altering, the rhythm monotonously repeated until one day, suddenly it changes. The next day you're shuffling along to a different tune like you've been doing it all your life, and you can't even remember what it was like beforehand.

This girl, this small young woman, had upset his carefully orchestrated routine.

Directly after he'd picked her up, he'd scouted the vicinity for a little more than an hour in the dark looking anxiously for some sign of wreckage from which to salvage at least a modest reward for his efforts, acutely aware that this unplanned fuel burn was eating into his already narrow profit margin. He had found nothing. Just the girl and her bag. She'd been minutes away from death when he'd knelt down beside her slight crumpled body. Each breath she unconsciously drew in was killing her with toxins and oxygen denial. He had hastily placed his O2 mask over her face and held his breath as he heaved her effortlessly up in his arms and carried her quickly back inside the shuttle. He'd gently laid her down on his bunk and swiftly launched the shuttle. For a few moments he anxiously debated whether to return to New Haven to drop her off there with the first port official he could find, or continue on his way.

A dangerously extended exposure to the atmosphere on Harpers Reach had a pretty unambiguous affect on any hapless victim. Either you got away with it or you suffered severe brain damage, a short coma, followed by respiratory failure and death. Returning to New Haven frankly would do her no good at all if the poor girl had sucked in two or three too many breaths. He decided to continue on his way. If she died during the night, he would wrap up the body in plasti-film and store her in the hold. When he got to the Oxxon refinery, he'd turn her body over to the one law enforcement officer up there and *he* could worry about what to do with it.

During that first night, he'd kept himself awake by flipping off the autopilot and taking the helm himself. He had come back from the cockpit several times to pour himself some coffee and wandered over to his bunk to feel her skin, half expecting on each occasion to find it cold and clammy and a corpse beginning to stiffen. After thirty-six hours she had finally come round.

He was relieved to find that she hadn't been reduced to a drooling vegetative state from brain damage when she'd finally broken her silence and asked if he had some milk.

It took Ellie Quin just the first day aboard the rumbling confines of the shuttle to grow accustomed to her surroundings. The bruises on her hips and the scrapes on her shins and elbows proved an effective aid in teaching her the layout of the cabin area and, more importantly, where all the sharp edges and corners were. She found herself quickly adopting the bizarre duck-and-swerve movement patterns of Aaron as he frequently made trips up and down the length of the claustrophobic assault course, either searching for a misplaced cup of coffee or making desperately for the toilet.

By the second day aboard she decided to carve herself a useful role and nominated herself as the 'Ship's Cook'. The role actually extended itself to no more than bringing Aaron a fresh mug of coffee every half hour and programming the FoodSmart to spew out something interesting to eat three times a day. Aaron had only gotten round to programming about half a dozen different meal templates into the protein converter and he had been dining on just these six different meals aboard the shuttle for as long as he could remember. Ellie swiftly picked up the coding language and tapped in another dozen meal templates. The pale, turd-like protein-paste the FoodSmart squeezed out still tasted pretty similar, but at least the new turds looked and tasted slightly different. It wasn't a lot, but it made her feel less like a spare wheel, and a bit more like a useful crew member, earning her passage on some exciting adventure.

During the fourth night Ellie awoke with a start. She felt one of Aaron's huge hands grasping her shoulder and shaking her in a way he must have thought was gentle.

'Wake up dozy,' he said in a deep rumble.

'I-I-I'm a-a-asleep,' she muttered, her voice warbling as he shook her.

She opened her eyes. The cabin was dark and she could only just see the silhouette of the big man leaning over her.

'Get up!' he said. 'Quickly, you need to see this.'

'Wha-a-at?' she asked, tired and reaching for his hand to remove it from her shoulder.

'Ellie, shift your lazy buns before I tip you out,' he said with a hint of exasperation in his voice.

'O-o-okay, okay…I'm up.'

Aaron stopped shaking her and moved off into the darkness of the cabin towards the front of the cockpit. Still half asleep, she pulled herself up into a sitting position and then swung her feet down onto the cold metal floor.

'Why are the lights off?' she called out. 'I can't see a thing in here.'

He shouted back. 'Just get up here as quick as you can!'

She climbed off the bunk and headed cautiously towards the cockpit. She fumbled in the dark desperately trying to avoid the hazardous clutter, holding her arms out in front of her to feel her way forward.

She caught a hip on a crate full of tools and grunted painfully. 'Can you turn on a light back here? Before I shred myself.'

'No, dozy-girl...you'll need your night-eyes.'

'For what? I can't see anything anyway!'

'Just stop messing around and get up here now!'

She finally made her way up towards the cockpit, pulling herself into the co-pilot's seat. But not before barking her shin on the repair bench. The instrumentation on the control panel cast a faint amber glow onto his face. He looked excited.

'Look out of the window and tell me what you see.'

Ellie wiped the sleep from her eyes and turned to look out of her side window. It was dark outside. She checked the time on the data screen above her seat. It was still four hours from daybreak

'I see...night. It's dark, so...a whole lot of darkness is what I see,' she replied irritably, still rubbing her shin.

'Just keep looking ahead.'

She saw him glance at the navigational display. The orange patchwork of wire frames meant nothing to her, but they grew dense towards the top of the screen, and slowly these tightly packed lines were drifting downwards.

We're approaching something.

She looked out at the dark landscape ahead. She could just about detect the rugged, flat line of the horizon; a black featureless plain below and a very dark purple sky above. She imagined herself lying down there amongst the dust and rocks, a cold, silent, unforgiving landscape of flint and clay hundreds of thousands of square miles of relentlessly empty, featureless rubble, and many thousands of miles from the nearest settlement. She reminded herself of the warmth and scruffy comfort of the shuttle with its oily bunk and its makeshift clothesline strung across the cabin; the omnipresent smell of coffee and feet; and reminded herself how incredibly lucky she was to be up here and not down there.

'Can you see it yet?' Aaron asked with a hint of childlike excitement in his gravel voice.

Ellie continued to study the dark world out in front of her unsure what she was meant to be looking for. But this time she saw something that wasn't there before. A thin, almost imperceptible, pale line along the horizon to the north separating the ground from the sky, so faint it only registered towards the periphery of her vision and faded to nothing when she focused her eyes back on it.

She looked towards Aaron. 'I see a pale line.'

He nodded, saying nothing.

Ellie watched as the faint line slowly grew thicker and brighter. It was a pale blue line presently, and as wide as her little finger. She looked at him again, an expression of dawning realization betrayed her. He nodded and smiled, taking pleasure in the look of growing wonder on her face.

'We're approaching the arctic belt. We'll be over it in a minute or two.'

'Snow,' she said aloud.

'Yup, it's pure virgin snow and ice, untouched by man from here all the way north to the refineries. I'll take her down low when we get over it so you can get a closer look.'

Aaron watched her as she leant forward and pushed her nose against the glass to get a reflection-free view of the rapidly approaching arctic landscape ahead.

It still caught his breath after so many years. The suddenness of the change, after so much bland rust-red, arid terrain, the transition was simply astounding. One second you could be flying over pre-terraformed Mars, the next you could be flying over New Europa's untouched arctic continents, the transition between two worlds in the blink of an eye.

He took the helm, switched off the auto-pilot and pushed the shuttle's nose down. She quickly dropped altitude and was soon skimming fifty feet above the ground. Ahead of them, the pale white line became a shelf of ice that loomed towards them. At the last moment Aaron pulled the shuttle's nose up and they swooped over the top of the wall of ice and all of sudden the world below was polar north.

The snow glowed luminescent by the light of the stars and the Veil. Ellie couldn't suppress a whimper of delight.

'It's beautiful isn't it?' he said.

'It's…it…I just can't believe there's a place…'

'…on Harpers Reach as wonderful as this?' he finished her words.

Ellie nodded vigorously, a smile stretched across her small pale face.

'Check it out.' He hit a switch and floodlights beneath the shuttle's delta-wings suddenly kicked in. The arctic world below exploded - an impossibly brilliant white, and the reflected glare filled the cockpit.

'Oh my,' was all she could manage.

'Enjoy it, because one day soon, maybe in ten or twenty years, it'll all be gone, and the only people who will have seen it will be you, me and the hundred or so people who work up here.'

She shook her head. 'That's so sad.'

'Terraforming is pretty depressing crap, Ellie. We take a unique world, with its own amazing eco-system and environment full of things you'd never ever see again on any other world….and we trash it all to produce yet another homogenized, 35-degree, O2-rich trailer park. It's not like anyone even bothers to survey new planets any more, to record how they once were before we wade in and redecorate. We just see another ball of real estate around a star and, before you know it, there's a bunch of enviro-domes thrown up and several million brain-dead dome-drones moving in.'

'But I guess we need more room…you know for more people,' she offered half-heartedly.

'Maybe we just don't need any more people. Isn't three hundred billion enough in this Universe?!'

They watched the dazzling snow scape race beneath them for a while then he snapped off the floods. The cabin was once again dimly lit by the amber glow of the data screens.

'Many years from now, you can tell your grandchildren that there was once snow on Harpers Reach. And after they've finished nodding politely, they'll cart you off to the laughing-house.'

Ellie smiled gratefully at him although in the faint light she was sure he would only be able to make out her silhouette. 'Thanks for not letting me sleep through this.'

'That's okay. Hey…maybe I'll put her down on the snow when we head back this way in a couple of days. We can have a snowball fight or make a snow man.'

'Snow *man*?'

Aaron sighed. 'It's what people used to do a long time ago with snow, back in the days before we got used to living like lab-rats.'

OMNIPEDIA:
[Human Universe: digital encyclopedia]

Article: Sub-space Resonance

In the mid-twentieth century scientists discovered that the five different Super-string Theories being discussed were in fact one, but appeared to be five thanks to minor discrepancies caused by an unseen and, at that time, undiscovered phenomenon. It had been widely accepted for some time back then that ten spatial dimensions could be mathematically calculated. The discrepancies in Superstring Theory could be explained only by *hypothesizing* the existence of an eleventh.

Today we know that to be true, and it is this dimension that is used as a transmission medium for Sub-space Resonance signals. This is the process of exciting *cunarks* through the eleventh spatial dimension; a process that requires an inordinate amount of energy. The result is a vibration that can travel any distance instantly and be recorded and decoded at the other end.

Since its discovery eight hundred years ago, Sub-space Resonance has only ever been used sparingly by a few of the most senior executives of the most powerful corporations in Human Space. It was also used on extremely rare occasions by the Administration to relay matters of utmost urgency.

To understand the amount of energy involved in having a short Sub-space conversation, it would take the energy required to propel a battle cruiser at maximum speed for one year to transmit a five second message. Thus, as a mode of communication, it was then, and still is now, highly uneconomical. But, perhaps even more importantly, it is a very insecure communication medium. You see a Sub-space Resonance wave never diminishes. The wave, or as it is often described, the echo of the wave, will exist forever once it is formed. This being the case, it would be possible, hypothetically (with an almost infinite supply of energy to hand) to surf through the oceans of naturally occurring resonance wave frequencies today and hear snatched moments of conversations held over the last eight hundred years. Many such conversations being held between the wealthy and the powerful, the rulers and the power-brokers of the last millennium, and every one of these conversations about matters of paramount, history-altering importance. These conversations would have been held briefly with no time for courtesy or small-talk; brief exchanges of facts, information, and decisions made.

The ether of the eleventh dimension must be a historian's treasure trove.

It is known that around the time that Ellie Quin left her home for New Haven, the eminent Genetic scientist, Dr Edward Mason was killed in an unfortunate accident. In the aftermath of his death a very disturbing discovery was made aboard the Laboratory facility of the Department of Genetic Analysis. A discovery so profoundly disturbing that records show a Sub-space Resonance communication was made between two senior members of the Administration, in different parts of the galaxy, only two days after the death of Dr Mason. Understandably there are no records of what was said, but the timing of one such event so soon after the death of Dr Mason can only lead a curious mind to assume the dead man was the subject of the conversation.

Somewhere, vibrating on a string of particle matter, exist the echoes of that conversation made many hundreds of years ago. We can only guess at what was said in this conversation...

...

..

.

CHAPTER 14

.

..

...

....Who knows about this?

Only ourselves on the ruling committee, and the man who worked as Dr Mason's assistant, Rowan Brown. He's the one who made the discovery.

Has he been taken care of?

Rowan Brown has been dealt with.

Why do you think Mason has done this? He was one of us.

He had concerns.

This could destroy us all, the Administration, order...everything. If this child is out there, it could already be happening.

Yes, we need to move quickly, but discreetly. I have arranged for someone we can trust to go to Pacifica, to study Mason's notes. If this...*creature* has been released, he will find it.

He's good?

The best we have.

Give him any resources he needs. Anything at all...

He knows he has absolute authority to act on our behalf in this matter.

How long do you think we have to find it?

It is impossible to say. It could be years, it could be days. It might even be that Mason never got round to releasing it....that it was merely a fantasy of his.

And we're certain Mason is dead?

There was no body of course. His shuttle disintegrated on entry. In fact, no bodies were found. It is reasonable to assume he is dead.

But we can't be certain.

No, quite.

Mason was insane.

I agree……

…

..

.

CHAPTER 15

The stay at the Oxxon refinery was for one night only.

Ellie would have liked to have stayed much longer to give her time to explore the extraordinary surroundings of the accommodation building and the enormous towering nuclear powered converters. The accommodation building looked like a large cluster of dark-grey cubic crystals that had grown over time to overlay and bisect each other. It was a chaotic construction of much larger, old-fashioned reinforced steel habi-cubes that had been bolted together over a hundred years ago, and expanded upon over time.

Inside it was a labyrinth.

There were many areas of the building that had been abandoned and were now no longer used and reminded her of the remains of an old weather station not too far from home that she, Ted and Shona had explored many times with their Dad. Although there were nearly a hundred people living up here, at its peak the complex had housed nearly five hundred, and it had expanded piece-meal to accommodate them over the years. Now that the refinery was approaching the last few decades of its usefulness, the team of engineers, technicians and support staff was being reduced. As they retired, or died of old age, there were few new people hired. Gradually, through natural processes, the head count was being whittled down.

Ellie had been surprised to find a few of the engineers had their families living with them, and had spent some of the evening talking with a couple of girls of Shona's age.

She agreed with Aaron to keep things simple and pass herself off as his younger sister. Both girls assumed, being Aaron's sister, that she lived in New Haven and quizzed her endlessly for details of the place. She had found herself easily concocting fabricated answers to all of their questions. Most of her knowledge about New Haven was gleaned from the toob, and she guiltily described the city with eyes closed, recalling scenes from the various dramas and soaps she'd watched over the years. Both girls spent the evening lapping up every detail hungrily, and had whimpered pitifully when their father had called them to bed. Ellie felt sorry for them as she bid them farewell. It seemed likely that the two girls, and the dozen other children living up at the refinery, would spend the majority of their natural lives there, only having the chance to move away when their parents retired or sought other employment, or perhaps even died. She hoped that at least some of them would have the opportunity to leave the refinery before they were middle-aged.

Aaron spent the evening ticking off the supplies with the Quartermaster as they were unloaded from his shuttle's freight bay. It took five hours before they were through.

They were each allocated a visitor's bedroom, a small tidy and spartan space with little more than a bunk and a washroom. Ellie spent a full hour enjoying the hot-water spray-pod.

Early the next morning, they had a breakfast in the refinery's canteen and Ellie caught a glimpse through the canteen window of the two girls making their way across the snow between buildings, wrapped up in thick coats and gloves. There was a small school unit that had once taught much larger classes with a dedicated teaching staff, now one or two of the mothers were fulfilling that role for the remaining children. She guessed both girls were on their way to this make-do school. She waved a couple of times hoping to catch their attention, but decided it would be best if they didn't see her once more, and trigger another explosion of tears. She felt terribly sorry for them, their lives anchored to this place for perpetuity.

They were in the air shortly afterward and heading south. By the time the light was fading from the sky and dusk was approaching, Aaron had decided to treat Ellie and had put the shuttle down gently onto the ice. He handed her a spare coat of his that swamped her completely. They both took O2 masks with them as a precaution and then Aaron led her through the back of the cabin into the freight hold and outside via a ramp down onto the ice.

As she stepped off the metal of the ramp she felt a crisp surface of ice break and crumble beneath her boots. Her feet sank slightly into tightly packed powder-snow.

'Ohh, this is so wonderful!' she cried. She sucked in a mouthful of air, savoring the icy coldness of it inside her. She held her breath for a while. It was dense, oxygen rich.

'I bet you've never sampled O2 that pure, eh?'

Ellie shook her head and then let her breath out. She immediately giggled with surprise and delight at the cloud of condensation billowing out of her nostrils.

'I'm a dragon, look!' she said, doing it again.

Aaron laughed at her.

He bent down and with his big gloves he scooped up a handful of snow, patted it into a loose ball and threw it with unintended accuracy at her head. It smacked on her forehead between her eyes and showered her face.

'Ow!' she yelped stunned and upset by the impact. Her face wrinkled with hurt and indignation. 'Why did you go and do that?'

'Snowball fight? Remember I mentioned that?' he answered defensively. 'That's what you do...you pat snow into balls and you throw them at each other.'

Ellie looked down at the snow, confused. 'Why?'

'It's a game,' he added to be sure she understood.

'Oh, I see. All right.' She reached down and grabbed a handful and molded it into a ball and then threw it gingerly towards him. It disintegrated mid-air and merely sprayed Aaron with a fine dusting of snow.

'Useless!' he laughed. 'You gotta' pack it tight, so it lasts the flight.'

Ellie scooped up another handful and squeezed it hard, the snow fusing into hard ice between her hands. She squared up before Aaron. 'Right then, I'm armed and dangerous.'

'Oh I'm so-o-o scared,' he quivered.

The ice-ball thudded against the right side of his head and he felt his ear throb with pain. 'Okay, I think you got the idea there.'

They spent a good hour skirmishing in and around the shuttle's landing gear, and despite the intense exertion neither of them once felt the need to draw a breath from their masks. Later on, when Aaron found he barely had the strength to stand let alone duck and dodge, he showed Ellie how a single small snowball could be rolled along the ground to quickly produce a much larger snow-boulder. Both of them were soon grunting and straining, rolling a misshapen ball four feet in diameter.

As the last light of day faded from the sky and the golden sash and the stars gradually appeared above, they put the finishing touches on a crudely constructed snowman.

'There you go,' he said proudly. 'Let's call him George.'

Ellie nodded and examined their work. 'Not bad. Doesn't look much like a man though.'

'I wonder how many more of these will be made before it's all gone.'

Ellie looked at him. 'It's really going to melt? *All* of it?'

'Yup. The denser atmosphere will trap the solar heat on the surface. Harpers Reach is going to become a much warmer planet before they're done up here,' he said gesturing northwards towards the refineries.

'Shame.'

'That's the way it is, Ellie. You can't stop it happening, all you can do is make sure you get out there and see the wilderness and enjoy it before the rabble arrive.'

'Instead of doing what I'm doing? Heading for New Haven?'

Aaron shrugged. 'If that's what you still want to do. But why don't you set your sights higher? See if you can find a way off this fregging planet, go and find some world that's just been colonized, eh? Another wilderness.'

Ellie nodded. 'I'd like to do that some day.'

'Good,' he replied, 'I'd hate to see that crappy city swallow you up forever. Come on then girl, we better start south. Time is money.'

As they headed back up the ramp, Ellie turned around in the doorway of the freight hold to survey the pristine white landscape one last time.

Beautiful.

CHAPTER 16

The next days passed far too quickly for Ellie. She had grown, if not comfortable, then at least accustomed to, the simple routine aboard *Lisa*. As they drew nearer to New Haven she became agitated. The city felt like it might be a daunting experience for her after the stuffy, womb-like security of Aaron's shuttle.

Ellie decided to contact Mum and Dad as soon as she arrived at the city, just to reassure them that no harm had come to her. By now, she guessed, they might have suspected she had eloped with Sean and contacted his family. In turn, his father might have been able to get a message through to him on the army freight ship and he undoubtedly would have come clean and told them that she had been intent on getting to the city. She wondered if Sean was already in a cryogen sleep and the Freezer on its way to the next planet. If so, then there would be no way they could contact him for quite some time to find out what he knew of Ellie's plans. Whatever information her parents had by now, she knew they would be utterly desperate with worry.

She cried quietly for a while, well away from Aaron. She knew he would see those tears as a sign that she was having second thoughts about going into the city and decide that enough was enough and take her home regardless. She was crying for Mum and Dad, for the pain she had caused them over the last few days; the pain she was causing them even now, and would continue to cause them until they received that call from her and found out she was alright.

I'm so sorry Dad, Mum.

She was going to call as soon as she could.

As soon as they landed.

*

Towards late afternoon on the fourth day heading south, Aaron had grown sullen and quiet. Ellie in turn felt nervous. They were due to arrive at New Haven that evening, only a few hours away. As the city drew nearer she felt her ambitious resolve to enter the city on her own weaken, ever so slightly.

Aaron pointed out of the window to his left. 'Colonial plot 452? That's where your home is?'

'Yes.'

'It's just a few hours in that direction. You sure you don't want me to detour? It's not that far out of my way.'

Ellie bit her lip, a small part of her, growing by the minute, wanted to say *yes*.

'No,' she answered quietly.

He shrugged. Ellie had shown him her citizenship papers and education certificates the day after she'd woken up. She *was* twenty, and was, according to the laws of Harpers Reach, no longer a minor. 'I guess I can't force you then. Although I'm sure you know what I think about all this,' he said reproachfully.

'I know.'

The pair of them sat in silence as the shuttle rumbled onwards.

'Listen, when we get there, I'll let you sleep here, in the shuttle, tonight. But I'm heading out tomorrow with another delivery.'

'How long will that one take?'

'It's several runs between Harvest City and the Oxxon refineries. Probably three weeks in total.'

She felt a shudder of anxiety ripple through her. *Three weeks...on my own.* She had been hoping he would be around whilst she attempted to settle into the city somewhere, perhaps even had an apartment that he kept that she could rent from him until she found her own place.

'Uh...right.'

'We'll only be able to set down in the short-stay loading zone of the port. That's outside the city limits.'

'Is that outside the dome?'

'Yeah. You'll need to go through Processing before they let you inside.'

'Processing?'

Aaron turned to face her. 'Their immigration procedure; you'll be given a medical, they'll want to see your papers and they'll want to take a gene-swab. It's a complete pain in the ass and it'll probably take you a few hours.'

'Can you go with me?' she asked.

'Sorry, I can't. It's for first-time arrivals only,' he replied. 'You sure you still want to go into New Haven?'

Ellie nodded uncertainly. 'I can't turn back now,' she added weakly.

'Sure you can. If you think the city isn't for you. No-one's going to blame you or laugh at you if you change your mind now. Trust me, the place is a crap-hole. I only go there because business takes me there. You want me to turn *Lisa* around right now and take you home…that's fine by me.'

She remained silent, imagining a tearful homecoming, then some shouting, anger, disappointment from her parents. And after that was all over, finally a return to the stifling routine she had been enduring all her life. But it would be even worse than it was before, wouldn't it? Much worse. This time her dream to run away to the city would be spent. This time she'd know for certain that she was there for the rest of her life.

'Listen, Ellie. When we dock, stay overnight on the shuttle okay? Spend the night thinking about it. I mean re-e-eally thinking about it. If you want to go home tomorrow, I'll take you home.'

'Can we stay in touch if I go in?' she asked.

'You better had. I'll want to know you're doing okay in there.'

That made the decision a little easier for her. She had enough money in her bag perhaps to rent a room for several weeks. If things went really badly for her inside, then Aaron would be back in three weeks time and perhaps then she'd decide to go home. But at least she would have tried it out.

'If it's okay with you, I'll stay over tonight then.'

'And use that time to think hard about whether you're going in, or going home?'

The thinking's been done. I'm going in.

'Sure, I'll give it some real thought.'

Aaron seemed to relax a little. 'Good.'

Ellie cast a sideways glance at him; his unshaven face, now almost qualifying as a full grown beard, his fluffy blonde ponytail that poked out from beneath his faded cap, dancing as the shuttle skimmed over a pocket of dense air. Aaron Goodman – most definitely a *good man* – was her guardian angel. She felt her anxieties ease a little. New Haven might be a daunting place to walk into on your own, but with someone like Aaron to turn to if things got ugly, she felt she had a fighting chance of making it in there.

CHAPTER 17

The city of New Haven appeared on the horizon long after the last light of day had faded. She watched the enormous enviro-dome appear as a shimmering mirage, pulsating and undulating above a cushion of heat from the sun-baked ground into the cool night air. As the shuttle skimmed the lifeless arid desert below at three hundred miles per hour, the mirage grew quickly, and soon she was seeing with her own eyes details on the gargantuan hemisphere of the enviro-dome over New Haven that she'd never seen on the toob before. The semi-transparent material of the dome, a reinforced plexitex sheath, was crisscrossed with a mesh of fine metal support struts that looked as delicate as the silk strands of a spider's web at this distance. She guessed, up close, each of those struts was as wide as a habi-cube and hundreds of feet long. On top of the enviro-dome, at its very apex like a tuft of hair atop a shaved head, she could see a bristling mass of antennae, pylons and dishes.

As the dome grew on the horizon from something the size of a thumbnail held out at arm's length all the way up to the spectacle ahead of her that stretched from one side of the cockpit window to the other, she could make out the foggy silhouette of the city inside. She could see the faint outlines of tall towers clustered in the middle linked by bridges, or perhaps walkways, and a carpet of lesser towers tapering downwards either side towards an irregular metropolitan skyline. Here and there, projected against the fogged dome, her eyes picked out muted neon pulses of orange, red and purple light that seemed to clamor momentarily for attention.

The shuttle rode up a small rocky ridge in the desert and descended a shallow bank that led down into what was the planet's only significant major geological feature; an ancient meteorite crater, fifty miles in diameter. For the first time ever, Ellie saw the base of the dome.

Where dome meets clay.

Of course she had always known the city was built in a crater, and from her perch on the outlook she'd known that on the few days the atmosphere was clear enough, she was only ever going to be lucky enough to see the very top of the dome. But for some reason, she'd actually never even seen it on the toob - a shot of the bottom of the dome.

Never.

It seemed whenever a drama or news story required an establishing shot of New Haven, the curving top of the dome was shown, or a long distance shot...but never the base of the structure. Ellie had assumed the enviro-dome descended smoothly into the clay and at some point around the base circumference a huge floodlit entrance existed with a 'Welcome to New Haven' sign above it.

In fact, the base of the dome was overgrown with a shanty-town of low buildings, encrustations of chaotically connected habi-cubes and small, single-tenant plastex bubble-tents.

Aaron pulled to the left, steering the shuttle clockwise around the dome, following the encrustation of the shanty town, drifting onto a southerly course as the dome and the scruffy sprawl below passed them on the right.

Darkness robbed them of most of the visible details of the haphazardly-erected conurbation and only a multitude of dim, pin-prick-lights coming from thousands of individual porthole windows, and the occasional garish holographic billboard, gave the dark proto-urban tapestry below a sense of congested life.

'It's like that most of the way around the dome. Refugees from Celestion, and other sorts. The people inside call that mess down there 'the Scab'. Nice huh?'

It did actually look a little like scar tissue.

'It's mostly built up around the north, east, south and west entrances,' he added. 'Then it thins out as you move around, away from one entrance and builds up again as you approach the next.'

'Why are these people living outside?' she asked.

'They're all waiting to be let in,' he said, shaking his head. 'Beats me why. There's so much room on this planet, but everyone who arrives here wants to pack themselves into New Haven. It's crazy.'

An approach-vector graphic appeared on his nav-display and Aaron looked up out of the window to scan the dark ground ahead of them. Ellie followed his gaze.

'We're approaching the South Entrance. It's dead ahead. That's where the port is.'

She could see in the distance, beyond the dark carpet of shanty-homes below them, a large expanse of smooth ground bathed in pools of brilliant white light. As she watched a steady convoy of surface-to-orbit shuttles were descending vertically from the sky above, like a wagon train from Heaven, down to one particular location on the ground. She leant forward in her seat to look up into the sky above. She traced the receding procession of shuttles upwards into the deep purple of the night sky, and there she soon spotted the dark profile of a giant interstellar freighter. The front of the enormous ship glistened, its smooth carbo-steel hull reflecting the last rays of the sun in its high-orbit position above New Haven, just beyond the atmosphere of the planet.

'It takes nearly a week sometimes to unload those huge things,' said Aaron, seeing where she was looking. 'It'll hold that geo-stationary orbit, slowly rotating with the planet to maintain its spot directly above the port.'

'Wow,' Ellie muttered. 'How many shuttles do you think are emptying that big ship?'

'Probably a hundred or so, it depends how much there is to shift, and how much of a hurry they're in.'

As they drew closer, Ellie could see one or two other low-level vessels, like *Lisa*, converging across the crater basin from other directions towards the port.

'It's busy,' she said.

'Not really, this looks like pretty light traffic. I reckon we'll get to check in quite quickly.'

As the port drew closer, Ellie could see the layout and structure more clearly. The main landing field was a giant rectangle several miles on each side, sub-divided like a checkerboard into hundreds of numbered landing pads. She noticed the landing pads had various colors, pads of the same color being grouped together in blocks.

'Do those different colors mean anything?' she asked.

'Red pads are land and refuel only, blue pads, land and unload. Green is short term stay. Black is long term stay,' he answered automatically. 'Getting a black pad is often impossible, or at the very least, a real bitch of a job.'

'We're getting one?'

'Green. That's twelve hours pad-time only. Enough time for me to get some sleep, collect up my next payload and stock up on supplies again.' He looked across at Ellie. 'I guess I'm going to need to get some more Solar Nuggatz , I noticed you finished my second box.'

Ellie shrunk guiltily. 'Sorry.'

Aaron grinned, 'don't worry about it. I'm still after the other Plasma Rangers. Maybe this time I'll get lucky.'

'Or you'll end up with two more Tracs to add to your collection.'

Aaron eased the speed of his shuttle down as they drew closer and Ellie returned her gaze to the floodlit spectacle ahead.

'Any second now we should come under the control of the PGS.'

'What's that?'

'Port Guidance System, it's their automated traffic control system.'

As he spoke the navigation screen displayed a linking chain icon, it flashed in the corner of the screen. Ellie knew what that was; an everyday icon, as familiar as a toob channel logo, or any brand of breakfast cereal. It was the AI handshake, one piece of software politely introducing itself to another.

The PGS queried *Lisa*'s onboard computer for remote-control readiness. The exchange of data was instantaneous and the handshake icon was replaced with a menu:

Landing Request:
[Red]   : [3 mins waiting]
[Blue]   : [vacant zones]
[Green] : [vacant zones]
[Black] : [2 days waiting]

Aaron nodded and selected Green. 'Good, we can go right on in.'

Almost immediately the shuttle accelerated slightly, the pitch of the engines rising and the nose of the craft began to pull up sharply.

Ellie yelped with surprise.

'Relax, that's just PGS kicking in,' said Aaron, settling back into his seat to enjoy the complex ballet of the vessels around them.

They rose steeply over the landing field, moving swiftly past other shuttles of varying sizes until the *Lisa* was over the allocated landing pad several hundred feet below. Then with little warning the shuttle began a rapid, vertical descent towards it.

Ellie felt her stomach float unpleasantly as they dropped, and a gurgle of fear and nausea escaped her throat. She gripped both armrests of her seat and screwed up her eyes as they seemed to plummet towards an inevitably explosive impact with the ground. She heard a deep throaty chuckle coming from Aaron. The sensation was short-lived, and seconds later the rate of drop tailed off quickly as they approached the green pad. Descending the last twenty feet, there was no sense of motion whatsoever, and they touched down with an almost indiscernible bump.

A moment later, the pad on which they had landed began to slowly lower down into the ground, revealing a small hanger

'Honey, I'm ho-ome,' sang Aaron with little enthusiasm.

'That's it then? We've landed?' asked Ellie hopefully.

'Yup.'

She opened her eyes and released her grip on both of the armrests. 'Oh my God,' she sighed, 'that drop was really horrible.'

CHAPTER 18

Ellie didn't sleep at all that night. Neither did Aaron. Getting hold of the freight he was due to take to the planet's 2nd city, Harvest City, and ensuring it was loaded aboard the shuttle had taken much longer than he'd anticipated. He watched the time anxiously as the night slipped away, waiting for a team of loaders to get round to hauling his cargo in. Then as dawn approached, with only a few hours left before he had to vacate the pad, he hurried to the Port's one supply shop and hastily bought enough coffee and protein-paste for the FoodSmart to keep him going for the three week trip.

He arrived back at the shuttle with only ten minutes left before the PGS was due to handshake his shuttle's computer. If he missed that, he'd incur a hefty fine that would double with every few minutes. The roof to the sub-surface hangar slid back revealing the pale cream morning sky above, and slowly the green pad on which *Lisa* was parked began to rise upwards.

Ellie was up, her meager bag of possessions packed and ready to go.

'Did you manage to get any sleep then?' he asked as he squeezed past her to get to the cockpit to boot up the computer and start warming up the shuttle's engines.

'No, not really,' she replied.

'So...you spent last night doing some thinking then, eh?'

Ellie had been awake all night. Not thinking about whether she was heading in - that was already a done deal. But nervously conjuring images of what it was going to be like inside the dome. Even if she hadn't been trembling with a mixture of excitement and sheer terror, the noise of the cargo being loaded into the hold and that of two engineers cursing loudly whilst they stripped down the engine of a shuttle next door, would have kept her from sleeping. She had spent the entire night whilst Aaron was out shopping and chasing up the loading team, pacing the length of the shuttle and mustering her courage to remain steadfast and not stray from her decision to head inside today.

'So what's it going to be? Am I taking you home this morning?' he asked hopefully.

'I'm going in.'

Aaron shrugged. 'Okay. If I can't change your mind, then let me give you some advice girl,' he said as he punched the engines on and they whirred to life. 'You go in today, and you give yourself a clear goal and a deadline.'

'A what?'

'A *goal!* Maybe it's, I dunno…to earn a certain amount of creds, or to do something like, to get a certain kind of job. You understand? Get yourself a fregging goal and make that your focus. Then make sure you set a deadline, maybe it's a few weeks, months, years, whatever. You hit the goal, then great, set yourself another one!'

He's talking like we're never going to see each other again.

'But if you fail, you get out of there Ellie, you damn well go home. Don't let this place knock you down and suck the life out of you and turn you into another one of those hopeless zombies in there.'

She recalled Sean's words at the Traders Show.

Someday, not only will you outgrow New Haven, you'll make it off-world too.

Now there was her goal.

'Stay away from the Service District. That's the rough part of town. There's all sorts there, off-worlders, rogues, bad types. They'll see you Ellie, and they'll think it's Christmas time. Do you understand? And don't trust anyone, least of all the Law Marshals. They're all crooked, dishonest, bought. If you get ripped, don't expect anyone to help you out, so just don't get ripped okay? Don't trust anyone. Now…'

She felt tears beginning to well up in her eyes.

'…there's no easy money in there. If someone promises you easy money, *run*. Seriously. It means you're being asked to do something illegal, or worse, some sick son-of-a-bitch wants to do something illegal to you. It's a frontier town in there, a lot of men, and not as many women. Most men in there want….well, I guess I don't need to spell that out to you, but you need to be very careful okay? Be careful who you get close to, but make sure you find a good friend, another girl maybe. The city can make you so scared you never want to leave your cube.

It helps if you got someone to be scared with.'

Ellie nodded. She could feel her bottom lip beginning to tremble and a single tear rolled down her cheek.

'You need money inside, you gotta have money. You have none, then, you're finished. You need money for food, water, air and someplace to sleep....and none of that's cheap. Crap, I should know. So you've got to find some work, pretty quickly.'

Aaron turned towards Ellie to find her crying. 'What's up?'

She shook her head, 'nothing.'

'It doesn't look like nothing to me.'

'I guess I'm a little bit scared,' she managed to murmur between muted sobs. 'You make it sound like it's a...a really dangerous place.'

'Hell-o-o-o Ellie! Welcome to the real world, girl. For someone like you, this *is* a dangerous place!'

She turned to look out of the cockpit window. The first shards of morning sunlight were creeping over the rocky rim of the crater and bathed the port with a warm crimson hue. Long shadows from the parked vessels, big and small, stretched across the two miles of tarmac towards the glowing dome wall and the clutter of buildings around the southern entrance.

'It's not too late to go back home,' he offered once more.

One of the display screens flashed a five-minute departure warning.

'I've got to go pretty soon, otherwise the Port Authority is going to start hitting me with a fine. Listen, Ellie, I'm not sure you're ready for this.'

'But I can't go back!' she cried, her voice quivering painfully.

Aaron looked awkwardly at the screen. Time was ticking away and there were a dozen things he needed to be doing in order to be ready for the PGS to take control of the shuttle.

She wiped the tears from her face and took a deep, steadying breath. 'I have to go in.'

Aaron nodded solemnly. 'Well then, you mind the things I've told you Ellie, and you make sure the first thing you do when you get inside is contact your family and tell them you're okay. Right?'

She nodded.

'And when I come back in three weeks, we'll meet up and you can tell me how you're doing. Deal?'

'Deal,' she replied quickly. 'Where, though?'

Aaron took a moment to consider that. 'There's a Slap n' Grill just beside the south entrance, inside the dome, 'Dionysius'. I'll see you there for breakfast, three weeks from today, okay?'

'Okay.'

Ellie smiled weakly before finally throwing herself forward and wrapping her arms around his broad shoulders. 'Thank you for everything,' she whispered into his chest.

Aaron held her awkwardly for a moment, one huge hand all but enveloping her narrow back.

He pushed her gently away after a moment. 'You better get going,' he said, 'I've got stuff to do.'

She reached down for her bag and squeezed out between the two seats in the cockpit making her way back through the cabin, now more cramped than she'd ever seen it with new boxes of supplies littering the walkway. She reached the bulkhead to the hold and opened it. She turned back to wave at him, but he was already too busy prepping for launch to notice.

'Bye,' she mumbled, wondering, for some reason, if she'd ever actually see him again. She slid her O2 mask over her face and climbed through into the hold, weaving her way through pallets of boxes to the open hatchway. She descended the ramp and walked out into the cool morning, briskly crossing the green-painted landing pad towards a set of steps leading down into the ground and a subterranean walkway to the port building.

At the top of the stairs, Ellie turned to watch the shuttle take off.

The ramp folded up into *Lisa*'s hold and closed heavily with a loud industrial *clang*. A moment later she saw the vertical thrusters fire up, blowing a gust of hot air, grit and dust into her face. Towards the front of the shuttle she thought she caught a glimpse of Aaron through the mirrored glass - some movement, anyway.

He's waving.

She waved back, hoping that he could see her.

The shuttle suddenly began to rise, the thrusters whining noisily. She watched it sluggish at first, but then swiftly begin to ascend in a straight line up to a couple of hundred feet, and then it swung around to the east and headed across the landing field, towards the crater's edge in the far distance. She remained at the top of the steps, watching the shuttle go until it was no more than a faint dot in the red morning sky.

Oh crap. What am I doing?

OMNIPEDIA:
[Human Universe: digital encyclopedia]

Article: Ellie Quin - 'The trail grows cold'

Historians attempting to retrace Ellie Quin's early life will know that when she's supposed to have left her home for the city of New Haven, details of her life there become thin on the ground. Years after her death, a number of denizens of that appalling city, people of dubious character, emerged to claim they had been close friends of Ellie's, offering sordid details of her life inside, that most probably weren't true. Many of these so-called 'friends' crawled out of the woodwork for money, in some cases, *enormous* sums of money, because, in the immediate aftermath of The Event, Ellie Quin was very, *very* big news. The News Media went into a feeding frenzy for a while, desperately seeking tit-bits about her, but as it turned out, finding very little. And it is probably for this reason that there is little reference to her name today. The News Media went on to find a great deal more to report on after her death, as sweeping changes began to engulf all of Human Space.

There exists today only one piece of evidence that Ellie Quin actually did go to live in New Haven. In the Smithsonian-Matsushita Institute on Galilea, on the other side of the universe, their most prized exhibit is a preserved DNA swab taken from Ellie Quin at the point of entry to that, long gone city. It resides in storage in a cryogen case, surrounded by the museum's tightest security system.

Until she emerges from this city some time later, there is nothing on her, nothing at all. All that exists is simple speculation.

User Comment > CrazeeBeeff
i bet its worth a bazillion creds. Imagine that? For a drop of blud.

User Comment > DaPrinz-ezz
my boyfrend sayz Elliz blood could have germs in it that could wipe us all out. Thats why its all frozen and locked away.

User Comment > Emilia DarkStar

on my planet theres this old story about a girl who was a vampire. I bet that story is, like, maybe a version of the Ellie Quin story. Right?

CHAPTER 19

'Ow!' Ellie whimpered.

'Oh don't be silly girl, it's not painful,' said the immigration officer; a middle-aged woman with a hairy upper lip and not even a hint of laughter lines.

'Really? It's not *you* who has to use that thing,' she muttered toward the Gene-o-Pass machine as she extracted her hand and rubbed away a small dot of blood from the tip of her thumb.

'Do you knowingly have any of the following medical conditions; Meningitus-Plus, Strapilitus-D, Carpolhungus Syndrome, Off-world Weasels?'

Ellie shook her head, 'no.'

'Any sexually transmitted diseases from non-human species?

'What? People actually...?!'

'That's a simple yes/no question, miss. I'll ask again. Any sexually-'

'No!!'

'Respiratory problems?'

'No.'

The immigration officer looked at her wearily. 'Well you will soon, honey. Okay, let's see your citizenship papers.'

Ellie pulled them out of her bag and handed them to her. She held them at arm's length with hands sheathed in elbow-length rubber gloves and placed them on a self-illuminated counter. She swung a large machine over the documents and a bright beam of light travelled across the document as it was scanned.

The Immigration Processing Center was a large open-plan chamber that looked like at one time it had been some sort of maintenance hangar. It was packed tightly with people who looked exhausted and defeated. Many of them carried with them even less than she did; some of them seemed to have nothing but the clothes they were standing in.

Refugees from Celestion.

She supposed these were people like the Quin family; people who had been strong and hardy enough to be amongst the first wave of settlers on that troubled planet. They had been prepared to brave the extreme environmental conditions there, as the rapidly-implemented climate-control system began to kick into action.

Ellie knew there was more to the disaster story of that planet than sheer bad luck and bad planning. The terraforming process had been undertaken by some large company like Oxxon - she couldn't recall the name of it. Normally, it took a couple of hundred years to tame a planet, but this particular company had claimed it could do the same work in a quarter of the time, some fifty years.

A quarter of the time, a quarter of the cost.

She noticed there were no children amongst them, not a single one. But then she remembered reading somewhere that first-wave terraformers rarely had paternity requests approved. The official line the authorities took was that an 'uncooked' world was no place for a child. The more cynical, like her Dad, suggested that the authorities didn't want the 'first-wavers' distracted from their work with parental responsibilities. On Harpers Reach, being a world where terraforming was well-established, the official line was a little more relaxed.

Amongst the long queues snaking across the hanger, she saw a few off-worlders who looked markedly different. One genetically-modified family she spotted had livid, orange skin. She watched them discreetly, fascinated by their skin color, their different body gestures. Against the background noise of the place she strained to listen to them as they talked. She thought she heard a few words exchanged. It was unintelligible, another language entirely but with a distinct melodic quality.

She had hoped that she might see at least one alien amongst the crowd, but today it seemed there were none trying to seek entry to the city.

'Okay, it seems your papers are in order,' the immigration officer said. 'But you sure as shuck don't look twenty to me.'

'Well I am.'

She raised a hand. 'Save it. The papers check out, so you're fine on that score.' She put a hand on her hip and studied Ellie intently.

'What?'

'You ain't going to make it inside, is what I'm thinking. You got family or friends in here to sponsor you?'

Ellie wondered whether the question was a trap. 'Yes…yes I have.'

'Hmmm, and the name?'

'Aaron Goodman.'

The immigration officer spoke the name into a microphone mounted on the collar of her dark red uniform. A hologram display screen appeared in front of her face and she scanned the details.

'What is he? An Uncle or something?'

'Like a big brother really.'

'And he's resident here?' she asked suspiciously.

'Mostly.'

'Cancel,' she muttered quietly, and the display screen vanished.

The immigration officer ran her eyes up and down her. 'And what are those marks on your hands and wrists? That looks like some sort of skin infection.'

Ellie looked down at them and then held them out. 'What these? They're tubweed stings.'

'Ahh, a farm girl huh? Let me guess, you've come to the big city to make your fame and fortune, eh?'

She scowled at her. The woman was mocking her. 'No. I've come here so I can earn some money so I can get a ticket off Harpers Reach.'

The immigration officer laughed. 'That's rich! Okay, fine. I'll see you then in a few weeks on your way back out again.' She winked at Ellie. She wasn't sure if it was a gesture of encouragement or derision.

'Well, for what it's worth, you're good to enter.' She stamped Ellie's citizenship papers and handed them back along with a small plastic ID card for the city. 'Don't lose the ID card or you'll be totally screwed.'

'Okay.'

'Oh, and yeah….Welcome to New Haven,' she added waving her along without a second thought.

Ellie proceeded towards a small grimy bulkhead ahead of her, marked with a small and easily missable sign. 'Access: South.'

'So that's it,' she said to herself, disappointed that the entrance bore no resemblance to the grand one she'd imagined passing through over and over in her dreams. Someone, sometime had sprayed a line of yellow paint across the floor in front of it and graffiti, now worn and fading, said 'Welcome to Shit Hole City'.

She stepped over the painted line and through the bulkhead into a long and narrow corridor of rusting carbo-steel plate walls covered in yet more graffiti. It seemed New Haven was doing its level best to discourage and dishearten new arrivals by presenting them with such a soulless and dispiriting first impression.

There were few others in the corridor and only one other person followed after her. The vast majority of the people in the hangar waiting desperately for admission and an invaluable ID card were being turned away for one reason or another. It looked like the city authorities were toughening their stance on immigrants now.

She found a v-phone booth halfway down the corridor and decided now was as good a time as any to make the call. She'd promised Aaron. The machine swallowed a depressing number of credits before it allowed her to tap in the number on an ancient looking keypad. She found herself hoping that no-one would answer it and she could leave a message. If Mum or Dad answered, she knew there would be floods of tears from both ends and a barrage of desperate pleas for her to come home. She wasn't ready for that, not right now.

The v-phone chimed several times before Ted answered. His face immediately lit up when he recognized Ellie on his screen.

'Hey Ranger!' she said, hoping she sounded cheerful and confident.

'Ellie!' he yelled, and then, as if embarrassed at such a raw display of emotion, his eyes narrowed. 'Oh boy, dogface, you are in big trouble.'

Not 'Ellie I've missed you' or 'I'm so glad you're alive and well'...but 'oh boy, are you in trouble'.'

'Listen Ted, this call's costing me mega-creds, tell Mum and Dad I'm okay. Okay?'

'You know they called out everyone to look for you? They all turned up and drove around out there for ages.'

Ellie squirmed with guilt.

'Mum and Dad called the Eltwoods and they spoke to Sean on the big army ship and he told them you were going to run away to...'

'Ted, listen!'

'...to New Haven. IS that where you are now?'

'Ted!'

He shut up.

'Listen, tell Mum and Dad I'm okay. Yeah, I'm in the city.'

'Double-cool!' he roared excitedly.

'Tell them I'm doing fine and I'll call again soon, okay?'

'Sure.'

The readout on the screen showed the call had already cost her four of the five creds she had pumped in. 'I've got to go Ted, this is costing me a fortune.'

'Ellie, when are you coming back?'

'Not yet Ted, but I will. Take care alright? And tell Mum and Dad, and Shona, I love them.'

'Okay.'

'Love you too, you little scroat.' She blew a kiss at the screen and found herself laughing as Ted shot it down with an imaginary gun; it was an old gag between the two of them. Never was particularly funny but she laughed anyway.

The call ended abruptly as the last cred she had inserted was used up. She had spent five credits on a call that had lasted less than a minute. She began to wonder how long the remaining three hundred and fifty-one were going to last her.

She resumed walking down the remaining length of the corridor. At the end she could see another bulkhead that slid open for a couple ahead of her. Ellie caught the briefest glimpse of the city; a bright, brash, gaudy, sparkling glimpse. She quickened her pace as she passed down the final fifty yards and broke into a jog as she neared the end. The door registered her proximity and slid open with a grinding rattle and she stepped out of the entrance corridor into New Haven.

'Oh my…' she whispered.

She stood on a small plasticrete plaza that overlooked a busy intersection below. The intersection was filled with mingling pedestrians, a churning sea of people. Most of them were wearing brightly colored city-fashion clothes; the sort of cheaply mass-produced stuff that would have Shona frothing with envy. The two bisecting streets below were narrow and almost obscured from above by a layer of free-floating advertising banners and holographic billboards. Tall watermelon-shaped tenement blocks rose up from the street and towered towards the domed sky, every available surface on them that wasn't a window covered with slogans and brand names, animated information screens, and more banners and billboards. She looked up and saw a dense layer of sky-car traffic going nowhere, grid-locked and hovering at an intersection four hundred feet up. Beyond them, still higher, she could see pedestrian walkways and what looked like a shopping mall with a clear, glass floor. And, beyond that, the buildings tapered off just beneath the ceiling of the enviro-dome. The whole dizzying panoramic view, from the ground to the very top of the domed ceiling, seemed to be bathed in a thick syrupy heat haze.

Aaron had mentioned that the south entrance side of town was up-market and expensive. Ellie looked at the chaotic scene, a riot of color and grime, steam, smoke and noise, and wondered what the hell *down*-market must look like.

To her left, down some steps from the little plaza, she saw the Slap'n'Grill he'd said they would meet at in three weeks' time. Dionysius. A small grimy window, fogged with condensation, obscured the goings on inside the canteen. Outside, in front of it, a scruffy collection of plastex bucket chairs around wobbly tables played host to a number of men who all looked vaguely like

Aaron; drab clothing, unkempt and eagerly tucking into the sort of meal that a FoodSmart could never hope to deliver.

CHAPTER 20

The man behind the plastic security screen already looked like he didn't want to waste another moment listening to her, and she'd only spoken five words to him so far.

'Sixty-five,' he drawled.

'A week?'

'No, a night. Sixty-five creds a night.'

Her face drained of color. The man leant forward to get a look at her. His eyes ran slowly up and down her like some lecherous security scanning device. He sneered displaying a mouthful of multi-colored gemstone teeth.

'I can do you a little discount though, bidi-chick.'

Ellie pulled back from the screen a little. 'Uh…how much?'

'Say, a little something between us that we keep outa' the books. Hmmm bidi-chick?' he said, sticking out a tongue riddled with pins, and waggling it at her. 'Booty bonus.'

Ellie's mouth dropped open with dawning surprise and disgust. 'I…uhh…' was all she could produce.

'Hey? Whadya say, does the girl wanna' deal on that?'

She backed away from the man in the cubicle and stepped out from the small foyer into the street.

'Hey! Watch it limp-chick!' someone grunted at her as they passed by. She watched the pedestrians moving around her, all of them irritated that she wasn't moving along with the flow. Ellie stepped back and flattened herself against a wall to allow the steady current of foot-traffic to shuffle past.

Sixty-five creds a night?

'Oh freg,' she whispered.

I'm not going to last three nights, let alone three weeks.

This *was* the cheaper side of town, the northern end, the 'Service Sector' that both Sean and Aaron had warned her to steer clear of. Ellie had spent a good half of the day fighting her way along the crowded pedestrian-only streets, following a grossly inaccurate map she'd found in a discarded 'Newcomer's Handbook', to get here. She had hoped that the price of a cube in this sector would be a fraction of those charged on the other side. They had to be, or she was in trouble.

And now she *knew* she was in big trouble.

Opposite her, across a sea of moving heads and handheld light-sticks, she saw a small boutique offering promises of exotic pleasure from a collection of off-world beauties. A sticker slapped onto the window of the boutique, read 'Alien Lux films, now in stock!' Next to it she saw a small canteen, no bigger than her own habi-cube back home. She decided she needed to take stock of her situation, get out of the crush of humanity, away from the deafening noise of traffic and bleep-talk, blaring billboards clamoring for attention. There was no way she could hear herself think out here, bustled and bumped by an incessant stream of rude pedestrians. The canteen looked like an oasis of calm.

She squeezed her way over, attracting a barrage of mostly unintelligible curses from nearly every person whose path she dared to cross. The door to the canteen opened automatically as she touched it, and she stepped inside.

A row of stools faced one long plain wall with a long shelf-come-table only a few inches wide mounted on to it. At the far end stood a counter, above that, a depressingly limited menu of items were available; most of them she didn't recognize. She ordered a synthi-caff from a woman behind the counter who looked liked she'd happily have traded Ellie's old life on a three acre agri-plot for whatever grim existence she tolerated here. She repeatedly asked Ellie if she wanted Sweetox in it, but Ellie struggled to understand her clipped, off-world accent. In the end, Ellie just nodded idiotically and smiled as the lady gave up asking and added the chemical sweetener anyway.

She settled down on one of the stools near the window of the canteen and stared dispassionately at the throng of people passing by. Most of them looked beaten by the city; beaten, expressionless faces, downcast eyes fearful of meeting those of others.

Three weeks. Just got to hold it together for three weeks until Aaron comes back.

The thought provided little comfort. It was like an acknowledgment of failure already.

'Okay Ellie, let's take stock of this tricky little situation then. Let's sit and think,' she mumbled to herself. She opened her bag to study the contents. Perhaps, she wondered, there might be a few things she could sell to buy her another night or two's rent.

Her 'goal' had changed dramatically over the last few short hours. No longer was it to make enough money to buy a ticket into space. Forget that. Now all she wanted was to scrape together enough money to make it through the next three weeks until Aaron returned, and then, that was it…she'd head back home with her tail between her legs and be thankful for the simple comforts of home once more.

You're pathetic Ellie. You've only managed to last half a day before whimpering for home.

She found a small zipper-bag inside her own bag. She frowned with confusion, she didn't recognize it. Curious, she quickly opened it and delved inside, pulling out a note scribbled on paper. It was a note from Aaron:

Ellie,

*Forgive me, I looked in your bag to see
how much money you'd brought with you.
356 creds!!? How long did you think that
was going to last? There's some more
money in this bag. It should be enough to
keep you until I get back. By then I'm sure
you'll be more than ready to go home. It's
a loan girl, alright? I'm sure your parents
will happily square with me when they get
you back in one piece.
Dionysius, breakfast, three weeks, ok?*

Aaron

She felt around inside the bag and pulled
out a slim wad of New Haven notes. She
quickly counted them.

There was eight hundred creds there.
Eight hundred…and her three hundred and a
little. That gave her a total of eleven hundred
credits. She quickly did the math in her
head. That was just enough to pay rent on a
cube for two and a half weeks at sixty-five
creds a night. If she could find somewhere
marginally cheaper, say sixty, maybe even
fifty-five, she'd be covered for the full three
weeks. Of course, she conceded, there were
luxuries like food that she'd need to find

some money for, but if she could get just a little work, just enough to buy even some protein paste and water, she'd at least live.

Ellie sighed.

This wasn't turning out to be that First Day In The Big City that she'd been fantasizing about for as long as she could remember. The city felt dangerous, not exhilarating; the people living here didn't fascinate her, they frightened her. But she was going to be able to afford somewhere to sleep, probably not that comfortable or particularly nice to look at, but it would be a bolt hole for her, away from the noisy, scary chaos of the street.

Thank you Aaron.

She peeled the plastic lid off the cup and took a sip of the synthi-caff. It was bitter and stewed but the sweetener, although she actually hadn't wanted any of that chemical-gunk in her drink, helped to at least soften the unpleasant tang. It would do. She placed the money Aaron had loaned her, and her own pitiful savings, into the zipper-bag and placed that back in to her own shoulder bag.

'Okay then, first things first, let's go find a room to rent,' she uttered, stirring herself to action. She placed the plastic lid back on

207

her cup and took it out with her into the churning hum of the street.

Almost immediately she felt a tap on her shoulder and spun nervously around, hot 'caff splashing from the drink-hole of the plastic lid. Behind her stood an exotic-looking off-worlder; a lean, pale-skinned man, with hair gelled up into stiff spirals and colored red and blue. He wore a bright orange puffa-jacket with, Ellie noticed, one of the more expensive logos embossed across it.

'You? Am need resting? Stay?' he said with a confusing click of the tongue between words.

'I'm sorry?' she replied.

'Am needing place. Stay. Pay money for stay?'

Ellie smiled, she understood. 'Yes, I'm looking for a room to rent. A cheap one. Can you help me?'

'Helping. Yes.' The man smiled, revealing gemstone teeth like that leering man in his booth. The bizarre, gaping mouth full of multi-colored crystals was still a smile though, the first she'd seen all day. Unpleasant though he looked, she instantly felt a small bond with him. The first person today to offer her a shred of compassion.

'I've been looking and everywhere is just so expensive.'

He raised a hand. 'Too fast, speak slow now. Do you speak....' He pronounced a garbled word she'd never heard before. It was a question.

'Sorry no, I just speak Old Earth English.'

The man nodded. 'Okay. So you speaking slow.'

Ellie tried again, this time speaking the words slowly and loudly. 'I…need…a…cheap cube.'

'Need, place. Cheap place. Yes.'

'Yes, I need cheap place.'

The man reached out with one hand and grabbed her forearm. 'Good, show you. Come.'

Ellie was a little taken aback by the sudden gesture and took an involuntary step back. 'Uh…where are we going?'

'Place, cheap. Go up for cheap.' He said pointing directly above them to a squalid-looking tower that over-shadowed the street.

'We're going up there?'

He nodded, clicking his mouth repeatedly. 'Up is cheap.'

'Umm…okay then.'

The man pulled her by the forearm across the heaving street, weaving adroitly between the other pedestrians. He led her to a recessed doorway tucked between two small boutiques selling wares that looked disturbingly like weapons.

'We go up, number 561, press,' he said drawing her attention to a grubby keypad beside the door. 'Press. 561!'

'Oh, right.' She leant forward and studied the grimy keyboard trying to pick out the numbers. And it was then, of course, while she was distracted, that it happened.

She felt the strap of her bag slide off her shoulder, down her forearm, and over her hand, all in a split second. As she spun round to try and grab hold of it, the man was off into the street with it clasped firmly under one arm.

'NO!!!!!!!!!' she cried desperately. Everything was in there.

Everything.

Without thinking she turned and gave chase, following the man out into the busy street. He was running against the flow, buffeted and jostled by those shambling in the opposite direction. She could see the red and blue spirals of his hair above the crowd and followed those, making equally slow progress as her mugger.

'Help me!!! He's got my bag!!!' she screamed into the faces of those she was struggling to get past. Most of them flinched irritably from Ellie, not wanting to have to deal with her, not wanting even to have to acknowledge her.

Shit happens, seemed to be what they all wished to communicate with a nonchalant shrug of the shoulders. If no-one was going to help her, at least they started moving out of the way more quickly for Ellie than for her thief. She was gaining on him.

He turned a corner into a much wider street which was shared by pedestrians, pod-cars and d-peds weaving effortlessly around them. The spiral-haired off-worlder scrambled desperately through the crowd towards a large yellow skyhound that had descended gracefully to the ground and disgorged about a dozen people. It was looking ready to take off again and proceed to its next stop, and he looked determined to leave with it. Ellie followed him into the street and quickly caught up with him as he was held back from crossing to catch the skyhound by a dense gridlock of pods, between which pedestrians were attempting to squeeze one by one to cross the street. He cursed angrily as the large yellow vessel began to rise with a roar of suspenso-jets, up to join the air traffic two hundred feet above.

Ellie approached him from behind. He wasn't looking around, apparently confident that he'd already lost her. She reached out for the shoulder strap that dangled below the bag, held tightly in his arms.

'Hach!!!' he shouted as he felt her tugging it. He spun round to see Ellie, his eyes widening as he recognized her.

'It's mine! You give it back!' she shouted at him loudly, hoping someone bigger and stronger might step out of the wall of onlookers around them and intervene on her behalf.

He tugged back at the strap. 'Leave go!!!! Mine bag!' he shouted in turn, realizing what she was up to. 'Stealing! Thief!' he bellowed pitifully as he hung onto the bag.

'What?! But it's *mine*!'

'Thief! Thief!' he continued, his eyes rolling with mock-fear.

She pulled hard on the strap, dislodging the bag from his vice-like gripe. It fell to the street.

'Hach!!' he said again with frustration and bent down to grab it. Ellie reached down at the same time and got a hold on the other end of the bag. As they both rose and pulled with all their might, the bag ripped open, scattering all of her worldly possessions onto the ground. She saw the zipper-bag fly gracefully into the air and into the path of a pod travelling at a fair speed towards the corner.

'Oh no!' she had time to whimper before the pod smacked into it and a cloud of paper creds billowed up into the air.

The spiral-haired off-worlder cried out miserably as he witnessed his booty floating to the ground and every pedestrian within grasping distance helping themselves to whatever they could catch.

The off-worlder turned angrily towards Ellie, he raised one of his hands as if to strike her, then after spotting a law marshal further up the crowded street, thought better of it. She slumped down on the street, oblivious to the thief's snarling abuse. She sat on her bottom, cross legged, her arms splayed protectively around the few of her belongings that hadn't already been snatched away by hands emerging from the swirling mass of pedestrians passing by.

Her thief snarled something that sounded threatening before turning away and disappearing into the crowd.

She gathered together what remained of her belongings; her tartan dog, Jonny, her voice diary, one pair of pants and a pair of socks. The rest of her things had been flung into the milling crowd or been snatched off the pavement.

Above the still unmoving logjam of pod-cars, the last few notes of her precious money fluttered lazily, waiting to be claimed by an outstretched hand. The flurry of activity amongst those pedestrians that had been close enough to make a grab for the rest of it had died down, and once more they all resumed their sullen-faced journeys, each of them with a little bit of easy-money in their pockets and casting glances of disconnected curiosity over their shoulders back at Ellie

She let her head drop and felt the last of her will to live ebb away.

It's all gone. All of it.

'I give up…I want to go back home,' she whispered to herself as she remained on the floor, lacking the strength, the desire even, to get up. New Haven had beaten that final submission out of her within only a few short hours.

A single note of money fluttered to the ground beside her. A five-cred note.

Enough for a single hot snack.

As she reached out for it a shiny leather boot slammed down on the note, pinning it to the ground with a long, thin stiletto heal. Ellie pulled her hand back nervously.

'Okay, okay…you can have it,' she muttered miserably, flinching as she looked curiously up to see what sort of pitiless person could happily take the last of her money.

The leather boot belonged to a shiny leather-clad leg; the leg to a lean, athletic-looking torso covered with a fine, form-hugging lycra bodysuit. Looking down at her, Ellie saw a hard face pulled into a frown. Dark, almost black, lipstick and a thick orbit of dark eye shadow around each of her steel grey eyes gave the woman an almost ghostly presence. Her face was thick with a powdery white foundation and framed by a black bob of hair.

'That was pretty spectacular,' the woman said with a husky voice.

Ellie could only nod. Her mind was still on that last note of money, and perhaps if she played her cards right, the leather-clad female zombie standing over her might just let her keep it.

The woman kept her heel on the note and continued to look down at Ellie, as if studying an interesting new species of urban cockroach. 'First day in town?'

'Yes,' Ellie replied with a weak croak.

The woman knelt down beside Ellie with a creak of tight leather. Up close this woman's face didn't look quite so frightening. It softened still further as the faintest hint of a sympathetic smile crossed her glossy midnight lips.

'Had a pretty nasty first day huh?'

'Yes,' she answered, fighting hard to keep a lid on the tears of frustration she wanted to spill.

The woman continued to study Ellie, her face was a model of sculpted porcelain, beautiful; the sort of face that could sell toothpaste or an energy drink, or in fact anything on the toob. It was a face, Ellie could imagine, that had probably never looked like hers did now - crumpled and blotched with anxiety and grief.

'Let me help you,' she said reaching out for what was left of Ellie's possessions and wrapping them up in the tattered remnants of her shoulder bag. She held out a hand to Ellie.

Ellie glanced at it uncertainly. The woman, sighed impatiently, grasped Ellie's upper arm and lifted her onto her feet with a surprising strength.

'Come on limp-chick, I think you need a little bit of patching up.'

CHAPTER 21

Ellie stood in the door-way to the bar, unable to take a step forward.

'It's holo-décor floor girl, it's not real,' the woman laughed and shook her head, her glistening black bob waving gently like the wings of a bat.

Ellie stared at the flickering volcanic landscape below her. A cauldron of lava bubbled and spat hundreds of feet beneath them. The woman walked across to the bar, seemingly across an invisible force field and waved for Ellie to join her. Ellie took a tentative first step, her mind struggling to reassure her that the convincing illusion was nothing more than an effect projected against the floor. The second step was easier. Ellie caught up with the woman.

'Totally drool, isn't it?' she said.

Ellie nodded. She looked around the bar. The woman had said it was called *Dantes*. The walls and low ceiling were flickering with the reflected fiery amber glow from the holographic projection beneath their feet. There were several small intimate booths around the walls. In the middle of Dante's floor was a circular bar with a solitary barman standing idle in the middle.

Ellie watched with horror as a small table in one of the booths suddenly erupted into flames. Two men sitting at the table and arguing intensely about something, failed to even register the enormous jet of flames that billowed around their faces and then rose to the ceiling lazily as a small, livid mushroom cloud. From another booth a few seconds later a second jet of flames spurted from a table and drifted up to the ceiling where it discreetly faded out.

The woman watched with amusement at the expression of horror on Ellie's face.

'Relax. They're just holos. Pretty tidy eh?' she smiled.

Ellie nodded. 'Totally...uh...*drool*.'

'Listen, go find a quiet nook for us to sit in and I'll bring you a little pick-me-up,' the woman ordered.

Ellie didn't feel like a drink, but she didn't feel able to protest either. She nodded lethargically and headed towards a booth towards the back of the bar. She made her way across the glowing lava, staring down at the churning sea of magma, and wondering how merciful it might be if the glass floor beneath her opened up right now and dropped her into a lake of real lava.

She slumped down on a couch that curled around the little table. Both table and couch were flanked on either side by sturdy chrome poles that flickered with the distorted reflections of the churning lava and intermittent mushroom clouds of flames.

Despite the deep volcanic rumbling coming from the floor, and some gentle background music, the bar was a surprisingly soothing, almost restful place to be. It was empty, she noticed, except for the two men she'd seen engaged in a heated exchange in another booth. Given the crush outside on the street, she found that odd.

She watched the woman as she ordered some drinks from the barman. They seemed to be discussing something, and she saw the woman point her way. The barman turned to look at Ellie and then shook his head after he'd seen her. He handed the woman a couple of bottles and said something to her that clearly annoyed her. She replied with a hand gesture and walked over towards Ellie with two small, red bottles of drink.

She grabbed the chrome pole beside the couch and swung round gracefully on to the couch beside Ellie.

'Why is it so empty?' asked Ellie, seeking something to open a conversation with.

'It's not open yet is why. Doesn't open until later in the evening.'

'Oh,' she replied, realizing there was no explanation forthcoming as to why they'd been let in.

The woman pushed one of the bottles across the table towards her. 'Drink up, it'll settle your nerves,' she said.

Ellie looked up at the woman. 'Thanks for…'

'For what? Buying you a drink? Big deal…you just lost all your creds. I saw that druck rip you off girl. You did pretty good chasing him down and fighting to get your bag back. Plucky. You were pretty lucky though.'

'Lucky?'

'Yeah, he was thinking about doing you some serious hurt. I could see his hand going for something he was carrying. Maybe something pointy, or worse.'

Ellie felt a cold chill run over the backs of her arms. 'But there were loads of people all around.'

'You think that would make a difference? Not here I'm afraid.'

Ellie looked at the bottle in front of her. It was decorated with a red and yellow swoosh, a logo she was vaguely familiar with, perhaps an ad she'd seen on the toob.

'It's a Spartan. It's good,' said the woman.

Ellie took a sip of the ice cold drink, and immediately felt it chill her throat and warm her tummy an instant later. The woman took a swig of hers and then with no preamble at all, held her hand out across the table.

'I'm Jez. And you are?'

'Ellie.'

Ellie reached out and held her extended hand. Jez recoiled with embarrassment and shook her hand off. 'What? Ew! No...no don't *hold* my hand! Crud! Everyone will think we're lebby-chiks. No like this...'

She held her hand out again and gestured for Ellie to do likewise. Jez then locked her thumb round Ellie's and then waggled her fingers. Ellie copied her and the pair of hands locked together by thumbs looked like a bird flapping its wings.

It looked stupid to Ellie.

'There you go,' said Jez. 'Pleased to meet you Ellie.'

Ellie offered a faltering, wary smile. Not entirely sure whether Jez wasn't in some way softening her up for some cruel scam.

'So, you're what? Sixteen?...seventeen? You've left home, run away from some dull outpost somewhere on Harpers Reach to get to the big city. Am I right?'

'All of it except I'm twenty, not sixteen.'

Jez's eyes rounded. 'You shizzling with me? Twenty?'

'Yes. I know. I look younger. And I know sometimes people mistake me for a boy.'

Jez's brow crumpled. 'Sweet thing like you? Nah, you're clearly a girl.'

'Well that's kind. I-'

'So let me guess. You've seen images of New Haven all your life through the toob. It looks like a great place to live, full of exciting things happening...and you wanted some of that. How close am I?'

Ellie nodded once more. 'That's me, I'm afraid.'

'And you came here thinking you'd find a job with no problem, somewhere nice to live and have a fine old time for a few years. Does that sum you up farm-girl?'

'Mostly,' she said, 'but actually, one day, I want to get off Harpers Reach.'

The smile that had been slowly growing on Jez's face vanished. She stared with an almost chilling absence of emotion at Ellie. The dark panda-like aura of eye shadow made her steel-grey eyes appear even wider.

'*Leave* Harpers Reach?' she whispered with a hint of incredulity in her voice as if the concept of such a thing had yet to be invented.

'Yes,' Ellie answered uncertainly. She took another slurp of her Spartan and immediately experienced the warmth spreading out from her stomach and up into her chest.

'You mean that? Right? You really want to find a way off this mud ball?'

Ellie nodded. 'I do. I've watched the interstellar ships come and go since I was a kid.'

'*Leaving* Harpers Reach. That's one hell of an *ask-you* young Ellie-from-the-wilderness. One hell of an ask.'

Jez impulsively grabbed Ellie's hand and held it tightly in a way she had protested about and found so embarrassing only seconds earlier.

'Oh Ellie, you crazy little frontier-puppy. There are so few people out there who have the gonads to say that – say they want to leave this world and explore the big ol' black. They just can't see there's so much more to this...this...this dreg-hole than the crappy little cube they live in. Everyone in this little city is dead Allie, they just happen to still have a fregging pulse.'

'It's *Ellie*.'

Jez's grip on her hand tightened. 'I've finally found someone else who isn't a walking corpse! *Find*!'

She took another big swig from her bottle and slammed it down on the table theatrically. 'You know what? I want to get out of here too Ellie! That was the reason I came to this poisonous pustule of crudge in the first place. But for some stupid, crazy fregging reason I...I'm still here.' Jez seemed to become distracted, as if she were sorting through some old memories. 'I just seemed to have forgotten why I came here in the first place. This dreg-hole does that, you know. You're working so fregging hard to keep from sliding under, you just forget everything else.' Her eyes focused back on Ellie and all of a sudden, she grinned like a mischievous porcelain doll with a wonderfully wicked idea forming in her ceramic head.

'You want to be cube-chicks?'

'Cube-chicks?'

'Yeah cube-chicks. Share a cube?'

Maybe it was the drink finding its way up through the bloodstream to her brain, but Ellie suddenly felt the first prickling of optimism. 'I don't have any creds, I...'

'Oh, do shut your gaping food-sluice!' she growled with a voice hoarse with excitement. 'I'll find you a job you limp-frimp, then you can pay half the rent with me.'

'Uh, but we're strangers and...'

'Right. Fine. Let me fix that.' Jez took a slug of her drink. 'Here we go. I'm straight, I like going out and hitting the go-juice, I like men... I like men *a lot*, it can get kind of noisy in my cube. Hey, I watch the toob, sorry, but I like the quizzies, the gamer-shows and the sopa-drams. I like eating cruddy food from fast foodies, I'm untidy, messy, I swear a lot and I leave crud-loads of hair and gunk in the shower-trap, and if you ask me to clean up after me I'm likely to say 'fregg off'. Okay? Now, I'm not a stranger any more.'

Ellie sprayed a mouthful of the frothy pink drink out though her nose on to the table as she snorted with laughter. Simultaneously, as if the table was sharing the joke, it erupted with a column of holographic fire that swirled and twisted around their heads and shoulders. Ellie jerked back in her seat and let out a yelp of surprise, spilling yet more of her drink over the table.

'Was that spurt of Spartan a 'yes' Ellie-girl, eh? Say 'yes' you dippy-frontier-puppy!' shouted Jez.

Ellie wiped the glutinous drink off her chin and nose with the back of her hand as Jez leant forward on her elbows, demanding an answer with an impish grin bathed in the flickering light of the flames that danced around her like a livid orange halo.

'Cube-chiks, cube-chiks, cube-chiks, cube-chiks,' she cajoled, her jaw working hard to keep repeating the tongue twisting mantra. 'I can do this all night by the way.

Cube-chiks, cube-chiks, cube-chiks, cube-chiks, cube-chiks...'

Ellie could have cried, perhaps even screamed, for joy right then, right there.

'Okay, okay!' She grinned. 'I'd like that. I'll be your, uh....I'll be a cube-chik!'

Jez reached across and punched her shoulder affectionately. 'Excellent choice.'

Chapter 22

At that very moment, on the other side of Human Space, a high speed inter-stellar clipper had just picked up one very important passenger. An entire ship; the kind owned by or hired by trillionaires for journeys to the very edge of Human Space to witness exotic galactic phenomena or hunt the rarest of alien game, had been commissioned by the Administration at enormous cost to abandon its current grotesquely rich passengers on a remote refuelling station and divert across several solar systems to rendezvous with and pick up one of their very best 'finger men'.

At that very moment; as Ellie Quin discovered salvation of a sort in the unlikely form of a six foot tall lap-dancer, this 'finger man' - Deacon - closed his eyes and eased back into the gel-seat ready for the nauseating sensation of the system-jump drive to fire up and kick in. The Administration had given him a brief, very much a to-the-point mission statement; to go through the possessions, the files, the scribblings of a certain Dr Edward Mason. Recently deceased. Apparently the old fool had quietly gone insane in recent years and decided to initiate a little unauthorized project. Nothing too fancy - just an attempt to orchestrate the complete annihilation of humanity.

They needed to find this 'project'. If it was in fact already out there - out of the lab. And they had to find it fast.

Before it *activated*.

To be continued…

In

THE WORLD ACCORDING TO ELLIE QUIN
(Book 2 in the Ellie Quin series)

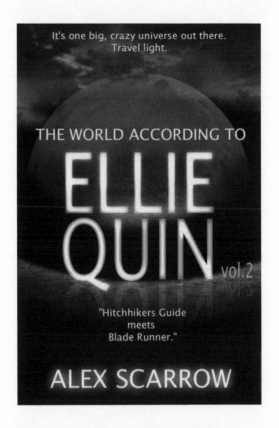

It's one big, crazy universe out there.
Travel light.

THE WORLD ACCORDING TO

ELLIE
QUIN vol.2

"Hitchhikers Guide
meets
Blade Runner."

ALEX SCARROW

THE WORLD ACCORDING TO
ELLIE QUIN
(Book 2 in the Ellie Quin series – available NOW)

Ellie's quest to escape the mundane life at home on the farm and explore the exciting city of New Haven begins with a new friend, Jez, at her side.

But the Administration's 'hatchet man', Deacon, is closing in on her. Will she escape the city and her home world before he arrives?

ALSO BY ALEX SCARROW

Time travel is already happening, there are already people coming through from our future into our past...and they are corrupting it, contaminating it. But, a small covert agency has been set up to preserve our history and our timeline: the TimeRiders.

Embark on a profoundly exciting journey through history with this nine book series published by Puffin. Available on Amazon Kindle, iBookstore, and in print in all good book stores.

3374689R00131

Printed in Great Britain
by Amazon.co.uk, Ltd.,
Marston Gate.